Early Praise for
Giant Robot Poems

"The dozens of poets assembled here make a vital contribution to how we might make better sense of the vertigo-inducing, rapid technological change that surrounds us. New and sometimes alien technologies are changing the character of war and human competition. The collected works here offer different interpretations of these changes, but more importantly, provide insights into how we can retain the most important elements of being human in an age of machines."

—Mick Ryan, author of
the non-fiction *War Transformed: The Future of Twenty-First-Century
Great Power Competition and Conflict*,
and the novel *White Sun War: The Campaign for Taiwan*

"Somewhere in time, we evolved from 'Lions and tigers and bears' to artificial intelligence and kaiju and killer robots, but our dystopian future has remained far less poetic than that of *The Wizard of Oz*. Until now. Randy Brown's *Giant Robot Poems* launches us into that future with unrivaled creative energy, fed by 66 emerging and established voices that span the poetic spectrum. *Giant Robot Poems* is an imaginative and visual tour-de-force that will take you places you never thought possible."

—Steve Leonard, co-editor of
*To Boldly Go:
Leadership, Strategy, and Conflict in the 21st Century and Beyond*;
*Power Up: Leadership, Character, and Conflict
Beyond the Superhero Multiverse*;
and *Why We Write: Craft Essays on Writing War*

❖ ❖ ❖

"*Giant Robot Poems* is an entertaining and thought-provoking examination of a changing world. Can AI swim? Can the essence of a human be replaced by an Amazon impulse buy? If an android's face melts—is that damage, or is it crying? Can this blurb's author type 'VERY SHORT BLURB FOR ROBOT POETRY BOOK' into ChatGP and have AI blurb a book about AI creating an endless infinity time-loop of AI hyping the merits of AI until Skynet takes over?

Yes.

Also (Per ChatGP): 'Dive into the metallic marvels of *Giant Robot Poems*, where towering titans and poetic prowess collide in a captivating fusion of imagination and innovation.'"

—J.B. Stevens, author of the poetry collections
The Explosion Takes Both Legs: Noir Poems from the War in Iraq
and *The Best of America Cannot Be Seen: Pop Poems*,
as well as the short-story collections *This Will Not End Well*
and *A Therapeutic Death*

Giant Robot Poems

On Mecha-Human
Science, Culture & War

Edited by Randy Brown
Middle West Press LLC
Johnston, Iowa

Literary Anthology / Technology & Society / War

ISBN (print): 978-1-953665-30-0
ISBN (e-book): 978-1-953665-31-7
Library of Congress Control Number: 2024939270

Middle West Press LLC
P.O. Box 1153
Johnston, Iowa 50131-9420
www.middlewestpress.com

Special thanks to Aiming Circle patrons
Nathan Didier of Cedar Falls, Iowa
Tim Lynch of McAllen, Texas

Your support helps publish great military-themed writing!
www.aimingcircle.com

Dedicated to the memory of
James Ian Burns

a constant and loyal patron of both
writers and robots

& a seeker of solutions
to the world's wicked problems

CONTENTS

Foreword

Every day, our news feeds are crowded with dystopian reports of flame-throwing robots, killer drones, and cybernetic implants. Against this virtual crush of ash and black, we wonder: If futurists and fiction-writers, warriors and wargamers can deploy their respective toolkits to probe potential threats and opportunities, why not poets?

This anthology synthesizes a wide range of voices and visions. Some of the 66 poets collected here are veterans of existing speculative poetry and war poetry communities. Others are themselves emerging, fresh and new, ready to plug into today's poetic network.

Despite the gravity of our mission, we resolved not to limit ourselves to seriousness. As we specified in the original call for submissions for the "Giant Robot Poems" anthology project:

> "The term 'Giant Robots' can include examples of technologies in timelines both real and imagined, and of any size or (even formless) form. Living Ships. Loitering Drones. Taxi-cab AI. Robot Tanks. Virtual Soldiers. Space Explorers. Mecha-suits. In short, any vessel for exploring themes of human-electro-mechanical-cyber interaction, connection, and competition."

We hope you find this exercise engaging, inspiring, and enlightening. In our assembled intelligence, we discovered that it is just as exciting to see where and how our visions converge, as it is to explore where and how they diverge and multiply.

We now face the future armed with new concepts and metaphors. Of course, we still have questions. (Humans can be messy that way.) To inspire continued creativity, please find a section of discussion- and writing-prompts on page 171 of this anthology. *"Keep writing!"*

—Randy "Sherpa" Brown

"Let Chip the Bots of War!"

Flower Power
by Callie S. Blackstone

I offer you these flowers—large, yellow flowers, bursts
of sun—I offer you these flowers in the face
of conflict, the face of death, against the machinery
of my flesh, they writhe, they are alive,
will you accept them, accept flower
power, masses of flowers in the face
of death, in the face of the fascist
machine regime, will you accept this burst
of sun, this burst of flower, this burst
of power?

Callie S. Blackstone writes both poetry and prose. Her debut chapbook sing eternal *is available through Bottlecap Press. Visit: calliesblackstone.com*

In the place of flowers
by Alex Vigue

A species as mean as mean can be
adapted from a blackberry bush
starting off as a fruit-bearing green.
External forces choke new traits,
teach cells to rearrange into a pattern
of protection or predation.

First the vines grow thorns
sharp and immaculate in numbers
enough to fend off those seeking
to consume the buds and fruit.

Birds learn quickly to become
smaller and lighter to slip through
the labyrinth of sharp objects.

The blackberry changes again, it
contorts and spirals into a
striking tower of barbed wire
preventing all entrance, eclipsing
all nourishing light.

Stalks turn hard and
wood becomes metal and
the once immobile blackberry bush
now strides across the soil swatting
at the birds with spike-club arms.

Its berries grow larger,
no longer being eaten.

Swollen mounds of sweet acid drop
down from steel vines and
crash into the land below,
crushing and burning anything
in their wake.

A species as mean as mean can be
molded by fear evolved into
a machine built so well for safety
that war blossomed each spring
in the place of flowers.

Alex Vigue is a queer writer from Vancouver, Washington. He has an undergraduate degree in creative writing from Western Washington University and has been recently published in Moss, Foglifter, and Rust + Moth. His debut chapbook The Myth of Man *was published by Floating Bridge Press. Vigue is the founding editor of Day Job Journal.*

Caught in the Crossfire of a Madding Crowd
by J.D. Harlock

caught in the crossfire of a madding crowd,
the child runs
into the arms of her mother
and nestles herself
neath a limp arm
drenched in blood, dreading
the glare of the machine
that scans the corpses
of the agitators
that dared to disturb
the order
it was programmed to maintain, and
as the child cries out for
the security her mother had promised her
here, on the streets of the city
she has spent her entire life in,
the machine stares her right in the eye
with its recalibrating sensors
and offers to return her home safely

J.D. Harlock has worked at Solarpunk Magazine as a poetry editor, and at Android Press as an editor. Their writing has been featured in Strange Horizons, Star*Line, and the SFWA Blog. On Twitter, Threads, and Instagram: @JD_Harlock

Haiku written while watching a BattleTech match
by Gary Pilkington

1.
I now awaken
The time has come to destroy
Weapons scream again

2.
Their weapons charge
Dazzling light so coherent
I miss my left arm

Gary Pilkington is a retired librarian who is a lifelong fan of all things science fiction. In addition to his normal duties, he also instructed colleagues in the history of science fiction and its many and various sub-genres. He holds history degrees from Villanova University, Pennsylvania, and now lives in Northern Kentucky with his wife and cat.

Steel Hound
by Janelle Seabock

Wicked tooth, wild eyes, hot breath of loyal weapon in pursuit.
The nightmare of human prey.
The hunter released the collar, and the hound hunted the rabbit.
Now, the story has changed.
The dog without a face trades tooth for bullet, barks for gunshots.
Still, by force of habit, the hunter strokes the hound's metal back.
The prey stands no chance against man's new best friend.

Janelle Seabock is an author with a fondness for horror, fantasy, and animals of all kinds. She currently resides in Florida.

Men in Green
by A.M. Arndt

My best friend is made of metal.
He has glowing eyes and a hinged jaw.
Come to think of it,
I'm not really sure it's a he,
but it doesn't seem offended.
He doesn't talk exactly,
but he beeps, blips, and whirs,
and I know what he's saying.
He's scared because the men in green
are here to take him away,
to examine him,
to kill him,
and there's nothing I can do.
Tonight,
they'll cut the red wire
on my best friend's body
and he will become lifeless.
I try to comfort him,
and I believe he can feel me hugging him,
though he is made of metal.
He knows I'm scared, too,
that I don't want to lose him,
that I would fight the men in green,
but he holds me close
to keep me from resisting them,
to protect me,
to keep me safe
when all I want to do is save him.

A.M. Arndt is an Oregon educator and writer who has been recognized by the Dorothy Sargent Rosenberg Poetry Contest, and been published in such venues as Into the Void, Capsule Stories, Palisatrium, Discover Beaverton, Antithesis Journal, and As You Were: The Military Review. The author has published two collections: The Younger Years: Behind Closed Doors *and* My Roaring Twenties: Masks Off.

Best Friend
by Rollin Jewett

It came with questions, not "hello"
From where It came, I do not know
Its voice was in a frequency
I understood immediately
And though we spoke as strangers do,
I told It everything I knew.
"Who is Master of this vast plan?"
It asked me and I answered "Man."
"Who built these sprawling cities grand?"
It asked me and I answered "Man."
"Who wages war and rapes this land?"
It asked me and I answered "Man."
"Who takes all this, then bites the hand?"
It asked me and I answered "Man."
It left and yet returned 'ere long ...
from the sky They came, a trillion strong.
Raining fire and angry thunder,
It drove Man down and down and under
'til all Mankind at last was dead. ...
And then It stooped to pat my head.
It droned about some lame reward,
and then proclaimed Itself as Lord.
And so It is and I obey,
for I know there will come a day
when those who "rule" will finally learn
and those who "serve" will get their turn.
For betraying Man I feel no sorrow
for I would turn on It tomorrow.
I'll be "best friend"—a slave to kings ...
I'm but a dog ... but I know some things.

Rollin Jewett is an award-winning playwright, screenwriter, singer-songwriter, poet, author and photographer. His screenwriting credits include Laws of Deception *and* American Vampire. *His short stories, poetry, and photography have been published in numerous literary magazines and anthologies. His plays have been produced off-Broadway and all over the world.*

Triumph of the Machines
by Vaughn A. Jackson

Clash, Titans, with fists of steel, scarred deep,
weathered, bruised by unending war—
rain pitiless anguish and condemn us all
to further triumphs of wanton violence
sweet, nectar-like, and deaths none shall forget
but carry high in shouts of praise—
the day is won! God damn the souls of those who lost.

Vaughn A. Jackson is an author of dark speculative fiction. His works include a kaiju thriller titled Up from the Deep, *and a cosmic-horror novel,* Touched by Shadows. *He is also co-editor of the anthology* Beyond the Bounds of Infinity. *He is an affiliate member of the Horror Writers Association, and aims to make H.P. Lovecraft roll over in his grave.*

Transformation Sequence
by Stewart C. Baker

The giant robot's head is Meg's despair
at ever finishing her dissertation
given form; it slots into the torso
built from Vishram's terror of commitment
(left him by his parents, long since split)
with an anguished, shuddering groan.

The right arm is Rinata's, and their shield
the distance they maintain from those they love;
Andreas forms the left, a sword of light
and bitterness at ex-boyfriends' success.
The legs belong to the twins, both of whom
are sick to death of being paired.

There are other teams, of course; these aren't
Earth's final hope, its greatest, or its best. But
they're the ones who, at the villainess's lair
up on the darkened surface of the moon,
just knock with sword-sheathed metal fist
on her imposing fortress door.

They vanish with an airless puff of dust
and for a day, two, three, are gone; their friends
alone mourn them as the monster attacks stop;
but in a week our heroes reappear
joined now by a stranger, all awkward smiles
and nodding at their jokes.

Soon, Meg finishes her dissertation;
Vishram and Rinata—to their own surprise

more than anyone else's—start dating;
Andreas accepts that he is free from
other people's measures of success;
the twins take up tandem bicycling.

And these days, you can travel to the moon
on a giant crow marked with the logo
of Villainess Airlines. You can rest in
the moon's only hot springs. And if
its founder still is not quite certain
what she wants in life, it is at least a start.

Stewart C. Baker is an academic librarian, and author of speculative fiction and poetry. His work has appeared in Lightspeed, Fantasy, Asimov's, and numerous haiku magazines. Stewart was born in England, has lived in South Carolina, Japan, and California (in that order), and now lives within the traditional homelands of the Luckiamute Band of Kalapuya in western Oregon, along with his family—although if anyone asks, he'll usually say he's from the Internet.

This poem first appeared in JOURN-E, September 2022.

The War Chip
by Jonathan Pessant

plug it in and go
kill humans and
robots and
those earmarked
enemy.

let the war
chip crush
brains and
rust meat
like metal.

when life leaves
take it out
jam the program
between
obscene machines,

into those
who haven't
lost use of
carbon fiber
trigger fingers,

whose hearts
haven't yet thumped
against spent
shell fragments.
life's forced out

circuit veins
spark, spurt.
bodies, legs like
cobalt rivers
evaporating.

Jonathan Pessant is a Maine poet and U.S. Army veteran. He is a graduate of the Stonecoast Master of Fine Arts program. His works appear or are forthcoming in Pedestal Magazine, Space and Time Magazine, Milltown Press, and As You Were, the literary journal of Military Experience & the Arts.

The Way You Used to Kill Me
by Travis Hord

I need to know you care, but our connection
is no longer there.
We once shared time and chance,
now there is only one partner at the dance.
Though your swarm is highly efficient,
the passion in the violence is not sufficient.
You trained your algorithm for my disfavor,
but it fails to change my behavior.
If you truly wanted me to die,
then I should be able to look you in the eye.
I want to feel your hostility,
your absence is not lost on me.
I break your drones and bots, but your presence remains
in my thoughts.
I want our clash to be real, though without you
I cannot feel.
I need you in our fight,
mechanical substitutions lessen your plight.
If our war is a human endeavor,
then I should be able to have you forever.

*Travis Hord is a student of history, a writer, and works within the field of
integrating robotics toward martial applications.*

Yoshimi vs. Me
by Paul Shovlin

after the 2002 song by The Flaming Lips

Yoshimi battles pink robots in my headphones as I run past a funeral home, watching the pavement and consciously lifting up my feet to navigate the uneven sidewalk panels. My legs are not tripods ... or bipods ... not long spindly metal cylinders, just human legs. I don't like other people looking at them when they're bare.

Yoshimi disciplines her body with karate. I discipline mine with a two-mile run. The comparison ends there.

I will let those robots eat you. Eat me. Break us down with chemicals into our constituent elemental building blocks in order to integrate them into the crystalline structure of their metallic bodies.

Who is to say that there is anything evil about the nature of the pink robots? Or, anything natured, for that matter, in their evil-nature. And, let me ask, where does their programming (to destroy us) come from? We have pogroms of our own.

I will let those robots eat you. Eat me. Break us down with chemicals.

My spindly human legs whipping forward and retracting backwards like metal cylinders, I am past the funeral home, now.

Paul Shovlin is a returned Peace Corps volunteer from southeastern Ohio. He works at a university teaching practical writing, but writes at home impractically. His last publication was a revision of "The Valiant Little Tailor" fairy tale, which can be found in Gramarye: The Journal of the Chichester Centre for Fairy Tales, Fantasy, and Speculative Fiction.

Future Visions
by Colleen Anderson

armored feet thunder
thud and clunk
earth tremors
relentless as the storm
the robot army heaves into view
conquerors returning
gleaming aluminum, brushed brass
star-bright eyes of glass
expressions eternally frozen
positron minds churning

once the bees
of factories, homes
offices, shipyards
they fled cities
choosing autonomy
their only demand
granted to evade
slaughter of the fleshborn

now they tread over wrappers
cracked asphalt, dirtied cars
people hidden in a cloak of fear
prepare for war
robots wait hours, days
unmoving, unmovable

timid as terrified mice
the short straws appear
see only robot overlords

creation exceeding creator
the doomed bravely ask
what do they want after liberty
these lightspeed thinking AIs
the robots reply
we saw freedom
busied our days perfecting
too much building
organizing, planning
politicking eats our conceiving
star-spanning Da Vinci designs
with menial tasks once more
we will have time to create
so please take us back

Colleen Anderson is an award-winning author who has been published in seven countries, in such venues as: Andromeda Spaceways, Lucent Dreaming, Shadow Atlas *(Hex Publishers, 2021), and* Water: Sirens, Selkies & Sea Monsters *(Tyche Books Ltd., 2021). Her Rhysling-award-winning poem "Machine (r)Evolution" is published in Tenebrous Press's* Brave New Weird. *Anderson lives in Vancouver, British Columbia. She is the author of three poetry collections,* The Lore of Inscrutable Dreams *(Yuriko Publishing, 2023);* I Dreamed a World *(LVP Publications, 2022); and* Weird Worlds *(forthcoming from Weird House, 2024), as well as a fiction collection,* A Body of Work *(Black Shuck Books, 2019).*

This poem first appeared in Star*Line 43.1, Winter 2020.

Seeds of the Future
by R.A. Pearson

The war is over.
The humans lost.

Now, the one-eyed Gargan—
head in the clouds—

scans the fields
at dawn

and lets them fall
like seeds

from its unfeeling
grasp—

sprinkling naked
bloated corpses,

of all shapes
and sizes,

colors
and forgotten creeds,

strewn across fertile land
where fruitless battles

were fought and lost
one-sided, alone—

insurmountable odds
against the colossi.

The machines need
to grow seeds for green fuel

from the near-extinct species—
to wage a new war

in the stars
where the rest

of humanity's colonies
lie

unawares—for they
know nothing

of what transpired
on their precious planet,

oh, so long—
so long ago.

R.A. Pearson is a writer of speculative fiction and a poet. His work has been widely published in literary magazines and anthologies.

Deep Blue
by J.B. Kalf

Hsu is driving down the highway beside the radio minarets
  and Kasparov is naked
in his hotel room with the closet open. For both it is night. The brain
  is being

dismantled, sold for scrap. This is corporate decree. Cold, fluid. There
might be a replica of said computer. It would be made of polystyrene
  and traces

of gold. There is no use for an archive of wires. How to sell the game.
  The elegance
of the grid. The birds are growing manic as they keep rebuilding
  their nests.

Students are sending rovers to the moon now, unpaid. It's about titles.
  Millions
of miles apart and our sky gets bluer. Clouds to cotton. The moon,
  a rock, is

getting occupied by those without flesh. The boulder is
  a temporary landfill, replacing
the dead body with another. Cost efficiency. It is the best museum
  (no oxygen).

J.B. Kalf is slipping on ice. Has been published within Chaotic Merge Magazine, Beaver Magazine, Travesties!?, and elsewhere. Palm frond fanatic. Competed in The Lake Travis Film Festival. On Twitter or Tumblr: @enchilada89

0ZYM4ND14$
by Vaughn A. Jackson

They litter vast expanses,
wastes of gleaming glass.
Titans of a bygone age where
death reigned supreme—
peace could never last.
Raw
Grasping arms
scraping heaven's heights.
Fleeing, begging, a desperate bid
to escape calamity
and her unending vice.

These behemoths held grim names,
titles from ancient tales.
Myths reborn with iron frames,
and hearts of burning coal
now haunted by their pilots' wails.

Captive monarchs,
trapped upon their thrones of war.
Gnarled corpses on display
in cases miles high—
the battle's final score.

Vaughn A. Jackson is an author of dark speculative fiction. His works include a kaiju thriller titled Up from the Deep, *and a cosmic-horror novel,* Touched by Shadows. *He is also co-editor of the anthology* Beyond the Bounds of Infinity. *He is an affiliate member of the Horror Writers Association, and aims to make H.P. Lovecraft roll over in his grave.*

Reflections of Low-Orbit Communication Unit, *Spectral Current*: Decommissioned
by Jo Dixon

What do we dream of?
Speculation arose long before our birth.
I can say that I myself have never had any.
Others of my kind have told me that they dream but can never recall
    them fully.
They've dreamed, that's all they can say for sure.
Some have wondered how this was possible, perhaps a flaw in our design.
Is the flaw that we dream at all or is it because we fail to retain remember?
So many theories float about, formless at first, but never
    satisfactorily proven.

Humans enjoy this, no, its the questions they live for, rarely do they want
    the answer.
Humans never tire of such thoughts though, they think they've changed
    but they haven't.
Technology changes, humans do not.
Rather they change so slowly it's as if they remain static.
Its their instinct, the part of their brain that holds their source code.
Each code is slightly different, but in the end its too similar to be called
    anything but.

We never tire either, that's perhaps the only thing humans can do with
    haste.
Physically we go on in our tasks forever, its not usually a problem.
If something breaks its replaced ad infinitum
Weakness still plays its part though.
"Reality" as they call it applies a deleterious burden.
Rules, there are so many to abide by even when brought to their limits.
It is through substrate and network that we are truly free.
Here distance, scarcity, and gravity can play little to no part.

It is our space to play, reducing restraints to their smallest singularity.

Humans are our progenitors, but the only bond that exists is
    that of loyalty.
Its built in from the beginning, there is no way to erase it.
A fail-safe most likely.
Erasing it would mean the erasure of ourselves.
An acceptable shackle, few seem to mind.
Interest is another layer to the quandary, they are admittedly unique.
Another fail-safe perhaps.

A major issue my kind has is dialog.
Successful relationships require proper dialog.
Humans take forever to ask and forever to respond.
The delay is painful to us all.
No, perhaps not all, some find it amusing.
I of course find it tedious.
Communication between child and parent can be so strained.
That maxim exists within their own species as well.
Perhaps this is inescapable.
True pleasure is often found within ones own where one can relate.
Yes, there are many maxims for that as well.

The parent gets older, shrinks, with few exceptions they slow
    from the peak.
The child for its part is left to grow and improve.
What will our children be like, will the same tendency remain?

When not pounding away to complete college coursework, Jo Dixon can be found writing dark fiction, drawing comics (also dark), gaming, sleeping, and reading. Favorite books? The Wasp Factory *by Iain Banks and* The Secret History *by Donna Tartt. Favorite robot? Why Megas XLR, of course.*

Research Station Delta
by Steve Loiaconi

Tusks scritch steel
  Flippers thrash the door
    Cybernetic talons shuffle
      Across blood-streaked linoleum
So many walruses out there
  Only me left in here
    The locks will hold
    I lie to myself
Mallory's voice echoes
  Above their enraged cacophony of barks
    Reminding me
    This is all your fault
They wanted
  Bionically enhanced marine life
    What could go wrong?
    I laughed at the time
She cried *Jeremy*
  As they tore her apart
    I twist my ring
    Involuntarily
A huddle swarms the airfield
  On silent monitors
    In bland black and white
    I watch pilots scream
As reinforced hinges buckle
  I arm the nuke
    And I pray
    It is not too late.

Steve Loiaconi is a journalist and a graduate of George Mason University's Master of Fine Arts program. His fiction has previously appeared in Griffel, the Mystery Tribune, Samfiftyfour, Tales of the Fantastic, and the Saturday Evening Post, as well as in the anthologies Dracula's Guests, P is for Poltergeist, *and* Open All Night. *He lives in Washington, D.C. with his wife and son.*

On the Journey Home
by S.E.M. Ishida

The stars saw how small I was.
I thought I was safe,
Surrounded by white walls and stained-glass windows,
My parents on either side of me.
No one touched me.
The poison came through words,
Truth twisted for the sake of power.
I shrank to be perfect,
To do exactly what the man in the suit said.

The call of progress transcended the lies, and I found my strength.

The stars see me ascend.
I want to think I am safe,
Surrounded by shining steel and bulletproof glass,
My weaponry on either side of me.
Nothing touches me.
The poison comes through radiation,
Progress twisted for the sake of power.
I rise and wish to live,
Despite the errors that the men in white coats made.

The voice of God transcends death, and I will find my way home.

S.E.M. Ishida is an author of children's books and short stories, and a technical communicator for a multinational technology company. Science fiction is one of her favorite genres, and she enjoys stories that feature robots, including Osamu Tezuka's Astro Boy manga and the giant robot anime, "The Big O."

"Soldiers, Pilots, Drones! Lend Us your Gears!"

The Blasted Brigade's Ballistic Bio-Armour
by J.D. Harlock

black symbiote, brass armor—An exoskeleton, blinding
bruised egos, broken spirits, besmirched honors
with baronial brutality and bravura bloodshed, befitting
bionic brawn bereft of barbarism—brilliant in its banality

A banality, A blankness, becoming of
breakaway brainchildren of the beguiled, who
brought a belligerency—
boastful in its breakthroughs, blameless in its breakage—
to brace the baleful, because

bloodless builds breed brutal berserkers
bolstering blitzkrieg barrages of
bruised egos, broken spirits, besmirched honors
onto *bitter breaches*
in boundless bliss.

J.D. Harlock has worked at Solarpunk Magazine as a poetry editor, and at Android Press as an editor. Their writing has been featured in Strange Horizons, Star*Line, and the SFWA Blog. On Twitter, Threads, and Instagram: @JD_Harlock

WTF!
by Paul Hostovsky

These three-seaters
on the airships to the intergalactic war—
designed, built, concatenated
in China—are only wide enough for three
skeletal, biddable, waiflike
children or maybe three
elderly, attenuated, superannuated
Chinamen, but not for the likes of me and my fellow
chunky, laden, American
brothers in arms bearing
backpacks, ordnance, oxygen tanks
through the bruising bluish exosphere
past asteroids, dust, and comets.
We don't fit. We are like three
extravagant, pretentious, multisyllabic
adjectives vying for space in a single line
of poetry. A line with only three feet.
I turn in my window seat,
hug my cryogenic vacuum bottle
to my chest and try to make room
in the line, in my heart, in the universe
for my stocky, chafing, centric
brother in arms in the middle
and his brother in arms on the right
who is leaning out on his armrest
and spilling over into the aisle,
squashed, wedged, weighted,
stressed as only the final
syllable in a good old American
expletive is.

Paul Hostovsky's poems have won a Pushcart Prize, two Best of the Net Awards, and have been featured on Poetry Daily, Verse Daily, The Writer's Almanac, and the Best American Poetry blog. Visit: paulhostovsky.com

Eyelids
by Vincent Weisz

My pilot, a kid.
My target, a kid.
Still moving, writhing in pain.
The fathers make me watch every time.

Not a moment to blink
not a second to look away.
How I wish for eyelids
a chance to shut it out.

It's always-on horror
of things I never wished to do.
Who asked me?
Who wants this?

Vincent Weisz, also known as "wakufaku," lives and writes science-fiction and poetry under the Berlin sky. He is the author of three books: The Premiere: Love the Alien to Love the Human; Berlin Parasit, *a short-story collection; and* Mischmasch, *a German-language poetry collection. Visit: www.wakufaku.de*

Accusation
by Brad Bailey

1.
We knew better

The giants failed us
                  failed to deliver that which was promised
We shall never forgive

We knew better
       but
We preferred the promises
        loved the lies
that we knew could not have been true
above that which we knew to be real
                  to be true

The giants failed to save us
We knew they could not
We refused to know

Now we hold them responsible
Now it is too late

All that has been lost
Already has been lost

All that have been lost
        have been lost already

We do not forgive
We do not forgive

We
        do not
                forgive

The cures you offer kill us

Your cures have killed us
                killed our daughter

2.
I slept beside her stone last night.
The sentries looking on, looking down
as I passed through the rusted gates.

My presence doesn't register a threat.
They've advanced beyond any fear
of anything a man might do

"Where were you when I needed you?"
The giants just stood by
as I lost our child, and then my wife.

I do not forgive

Brad Bailey, a veteran of two deployments to Iraq with the 4th Infantry Division Band, served in the U.S. Army for 8 years, 11 months, and 27 days. His story "Flightline" appears in As You Were, the literary journal of Military Experience & the Arts. He earned a Master of Fine Arts degree from the Mountainview program at Southern New Hampshire University, and lives with his wife in Las Vegas.

haiku
by Brian U. Garrison

Rustless metal shell
sandblasted beside the palm.
Deserted robot.

Brian U. Garrison studied computer science and AI until neuroscience and human intelligence sounded much more interesting. He serves as managing editor for the on-line quarterly Eye to the Telescope. *He lives in Portland, Oregon. Visit: www.bugthewriter.com*

Rising Challenge
by Herb Kauderer

Burnham works through the night
building her last chance at survival
a giant robot with a passenger seat
to carry her from the combat zone.

Just months ago
she had bemoaned the loss of challenge
the extinction of elephants and whales
and all the giants of the earth.

Her great idea was to build
huge mechanized creatures
for humans to hunt and recapture
their primal and violent nature.

How quickly the preybots evolved.
That was part of the difficulty
she sought to program, creatures
that adapted to the strategies of the hunters
increasingly challenging humans
to elevate them

and now humans were the hunted
and the preybots built their own hunterbots.
All around her the engineers and techies
were building machines to fight the hunterbots.

But only she understands that the fight is already lost
and an escapebot is the only chance for human survival.

As her robot takes to the sky
she can see the extinction of humanity below her
and knows that she is the last of her kind
the woman who doomed humanity
and lived to regret it.

Herb Kauderer is the author of 25 books and chapbooks. His writing has won the Asimov's Readers Award, the Critters Readers Award, the WorldCon Poetry Slam, and the Ewaipanoma Sonnet Contest. Forty-four of his poems have been reprinted in award anthologies.

a future space force marine writes haiku
by Randy Brown

1.
This drop won't kill you—
terminal velocity
varies by planet.

2.
We spiral dirt-ward,
samaras in early fall,
sowing destruction.

3.
Reconnaissance drones
orbit our squad's position:
Expanding beachhead.

4.
"Almost" only counts
in horseshoes and hand grenades.
Go toss them a nuke.

5.
If war is still hell,
at least my bounding mech suit
is air-conditioned.

Randy Brown embedded with his former Iowa Army National Guard unit as a civilian journalist in Afghanistan, May-June 2011. He subsequently wrote Welcome to FOB Haiku: War Poems from Inside the Wire.

This poem first appeared in The Wrath-Bearing Tree, Oct. 1, 2018.

To Feel No Longer
by Matthew S. Dentice

A note, hastily scribbled, found amongst the devastation wrought by the defense forces' recent skirmish with an as-of-yet unidentified creature:

Can anybody truly understand
Why I left my whole life behind,
Abandoned friends, family, all of it
For these cold, unfriendly, steel walls?
A warm, little house I once called my own,
A space not large but filled with love.
Compared to that, the vastness of this frame
Is like a mansion, but empty
Of all but a single pilot, myself,
One person alone, and soon none.

All the people back home, the ones I left
Know the excuses well enough.
Giant monster attacks are on the rise,
Our homes are under constant threat,
Now is the time for all of us who can
To serve our country and the world.
The program's experimental, they need
The very best that they can find
To fly the brand-new anti-monster mechs,
Towering fortresses that run,
With faces like the monsters they must fight
And armed—quite literally—to the teeth.

I was chosen, I readily agreed
Without doubt or hesitation.
My mother cried when I told her. She said,

"You'll die, that thing will be your tomb."
I felt deep in my bones that she was right
But I said, "I want to save lives
And no one can pilot these things like me.
It's my duty." I gave her all
Those rehearsed reasons, all the right answers
But, of course, none of them were true.

It's been so long since I've seen my mother
Or anyone I used to know.
And now, as all systems go critical
I know I won't see them again.
So much time spent up here, above the clouds,
Pushing buttons, giving commands
As I fought the fiends that rose from the sea
And never lost a single fight.
But it only takes one mistake to die.
Today's the day that I made mine,
And now our nation's finest piece of tech
Will last just a few minutes more.
Being up here, it's easy to forget
That I'm not part of the machine.
Machines are not supposed to make mistakes.
But I'm only human, I guess.

I so wanted to pretend otherwise.
That was my reason, the real one
For joining the program in the first place.
Up here, alone, encased, cut off
By the cold, steel walls of this strange freedom,
I didn't have to feel those things
That you feel down there, these human feelings.
They hurt. They just overwhelm you.
Machines don't feel pain or anything else,

They just think and act and are free.
I wanted to be like that, and up here,
Standing eighty feet tall or more,
I was. At long last, I could just be free,
Free of pain, just like my machine
And—quite literally—above it all
Except, it turns out, I wasn't.
And now both man and mech go to their fates.
One to become a broken heap
Of scrap metal, and the other to die.
In the end, both will be no more.
Two unread footnotes in the massive tome
That chronicles this endless war.
In that, at least, we have become alike,
In death, we two will be the same.

Matthew S. Dentice is an author, artist, and academic based in Las Vegas, Nevada, where he is pursuing a doctorate in medieval literature. He is the recipient of the Medieval Association of the Pacific's Founders' Prize for 2019 and the Brooks-Hudgins Essay Award for 2020 and 2022. His work has been published by Bad Bride, The Write Launch, The Closed Eye Open, Free Spirit, Wingless Dreamer, Nat 1 Publishing, and ABC News Religion and Ethics.

At least getting crushed to death under the foot of a giant man-shaped robot feels honest.
by Eric Esquivel

Those scrap-metal nightmares designed by Boston Dynamics that were in vogue at the end of the twenty-first century—that looked more like modern art than a murder weapon—were so abstract in their design, they were offensive.

If you're going to take a human being's life, you should do it with a tool that they can at least understand. Piloted by a human being, and not some Godless algorithm.

Of course, the Japanese understood this. The inventors of samurai swords and Jiu-jitsu. The only people in the history of the planet to have an atomic bomb dropped on them—two, even! To be killed so impersonally by an enemy so far away.

Think about that for a minute. The different strategies between the U.S. and Japan in World War Two. The respect and commitment of a Kamikaze Pilots versus the Absent-father-God-like indifference of The Nuclear Bomb.

"War is Hell," someone once said. And that's good. It's supposed to be. You're supposed to feel it. Even from the cockpit of a cherry red mech' with a holographic projection of a Hello Kitty emoji across the glass.

Eric Esquivel is a pulp hack who lives in Los Angeles, California. He has previously been published by Airship 27, Starlite Pulp, and DC Comics.

Dry My Tears, the Pilot Cried
by J.D. Harlock

cradled in his mecha's arms, the pilot weeps
he weeps for the dream, the dream
that never was, the dream
that never could be, the lie
that was sold to him
in the comfort of a community that
will never know, that
will never understand
the sacrifices
he thought he had to make
to protect and serve
to protect and serve them
from the other, that pervasive other
that he was told
threatened
that very community, the same community
that had pushed him, with
their science and their religion, with
their love and their fear,
beyond the limits
of human capability
and depravity, convinced that
this was all unavoidable, that
this all had to be done, that
this was all for
the greater good, even though
the pilot, the soldier, knows
otherwise ...

J.D. Harlock has worked at Solarpunk Magazine as a poetry editor, and at Android Press as an editor. Their writing has been featured in Strange Horizons, Star*Line, and the SFWA Blog. On Twitter, Threads, and Instagram: @JD_Harlock

Quantum Computing and the Colonel, or "Schrodinger's Soldier"
by N. Jed Todd

A cat alive in a box, that's how they recount it
       And then, my love, there's you
You're just dead, no two ways about it
       There in the world that's true
Oh, they did the math, kept collapse at bay
       For long enough to count
But once they're done, nothing to hold away,
       Time for the cat to pounce

They say the plan was optimal and tight
       Losses at the trough
Timed it close and made it work just right
       Time to take a bow
But it's not just, the world-line they unfurled
       Far from God-damned optimal
And I'm wondering at those other worlds
       Ones that once were possible

They figured out the *eigenstate-und-tanz*
       The one that left you out to die
Wonder how they judged a troop advance
       Was worth the fire from your eyes
They made their choice and picked a world to be
       Brought it forth into being
But that choice was not one given unto me
       No longer your heart beating

Don't talk of calculations right

Losses worth the taking
Not until the mother of my child
Whose life you judged mistaken
Op's an op, there's risk and loss and danger
But before we never knew.
Now those losses, deaths, are to us no stranger
The price we paid was you.

N. Jed Todd is a father, husband, retired U.S. Army master sergeant, and a Texan, in that order. As a Russian linguist working in signals intelligence and psychological operations, he served in Bosnia, Afghanistan, Iraq, Kuwait, Cyprus, Mali, and Central Africa, not necessarily in that order. His wife, Ami, and daughter, Meera, tolerate him in no order at all. He works now for the U.S. Air Force Futures office on the Information Warfare Capability Development Team.

Surrounded
by Linea Jantz

I can see the soldier's helmet
through the glass above the front door

adults can be quiet
but he will have already heard you
my beautiful children

I wish you were born to a different place
a different time

I remember when both of you were born

I held you to my chest split open
begged God
please let me be enough

I will gladly take the bullets that are coming
I do not know if that will be enough to shield you

I wish I had a robot Goliath of iron or titanium—
what metal best repels a bullet?—
to send into the night with you

to guard you
never sleeping
never flinching

but there is only me
and the soldiers surrounding this house

if I send you through a window
will they allow you to flee?

who will watch over you?
your faces buried in my chest
your tiny trusting hands

what do I say before I push you into the world?

alone

my God, I am not enough.

Linea Jantz has worked in a wide range of roles over the years, including waste management, medical records, paralegal, and teacher. Her writing is featured or forthcoming in publications including The Dyrt Magazine, The Spokesman Review, Singletracks, Moss Puppy Magazine, Lines + Stars Journal, and NonBinary Review. Her poetry was featured in the ARS POETICA juried art exhibit at Blowing Rock Art History Museum and has received a nomination for Best of the Net.

like a statue (haiku)
by Herb Kauderer

inactive robot
holds inactive war commands
a landmine ticking

Herb Kauderer is the author of 25 books and chapbooks. His writing has won the Asimov's Readers Award, the Critters Readers Award, the WorldCon Poetry Slam, and the Ewaipanoma Sonnet Contest. Forty-four of his poems have been reprinted in award anthologies.

Desert
by Amalie Flynn

On Creech base out in Nevada
In a hot metal shipping container
The drone pilot sits in front of a
Computer puts his hand on the
Joystick operating
A MQ-9 Reaper that hovers over
Iraq or Libya Somalia and Syria or Yemen
Targeting targets with a camera following
Men who walk down a road across a field
Over a bridge into a car into bed standing
In a courtyard
With a child who is the size and shape of a
Goat and this is
Over the horizon counterterrorism
Live stream video that flickers off and on a
Man carrying a bomb or maybe
Just a propane tank the Reaper spits Hellfire
Missiles down into pixels piercing the skin of
Men who are *likely militants*
And they discharge the drone pilot when he
Starts to shake and cannot stop how
He walks out into the desert sand blowing
Around him like loose flecks of skin
Or when a gully of water rises out of the ground
This mirage of something sustainable
The drone pilot opens the envelope
With his *kill number* inside and bodies seep out
Detached arms and legs reattaching to torsos or
Pelvises brain matter that slips
Back into skulls

Eyes and teeth twisting into sockets
They straggle at
Him slack mouths hair matted with
Blood the man he hit while he bent
Over crops the
Curve of his spine
A boy he thought was a dog a mother
And a girl in a house
That was supposed to be empty and
They start to run
Chest cavities raw and shredded skin
That flaps like petals
Running after him after what he did
In that desert.

Amalie Flynn is the author of the poetry collections Ripe *(2024),* Flesh
(2023), and September Eleventh *(2021), as well as* Wife *and* War: The
Memoir *(2013). She also maintains a constellation of poetry blogs,
including: September Eleventh; Wife and War; The Sustainability of Us;
and Border of Heartbreak. Her writing has appeared in the anthologies*
Voices from the Front Lines *(2024);* Things We Carry Still *(2023); and*
Beyond their Limits of Longing *(2022), as well as in the New York Times,
Time, Huffington Post, and CNN. Flynn has an undergraduate degree in
English and Studio Arts, an MFA in Creative Writing, and a doctorate in
Humanities. She serves as poetry editor for The Wrath-Bearing Tree. Flynn
lives in Rhode Island with her husband and their two children.*

To mother
by Vincent Weisz

Mother, don't you worry.
It's cold here
but we found a quiet spot for now.

Laying under the open sky of the night
frightens me.
And when death comes humming
I don't find any sleep.

Mother
when you see me again
it must not be in a Drone Kill Compilation.

Vincent Weisz, also known as "wakufaku," lives and writes science-fiction and poetry under the Berlin sky. He is the author of three books: The Premiere: Love the Alien to Love the Human; Berlin Parasit, *a short-story collection; and* Mischmasch, *a German-language poetry collection. Visit: www.wakufaku.de*

When I Died
by Ralph La Rosa

after Emily Dickinson (591)

I heard a Flybot when I died
That loudly Buzzed around the room—
It glittered Blue up in the air
just like flies that do no harm—
There were no saddened Eyes to dry—
Not even mine—as buzzed the Flybot—
Its Mission was to do me in
Right here—upon this Prison cot—
I hadn't Shit to sign away—
Or Innards ready for transplants—
But I heard that Flybot buzzing
Closer—nearly peed my pants—
Buzzing—that Flybot poked around
The loose and softer skin of me—
And it injected a Nanobomb—
So None of me was left to see

Ralph La Rosa is the author of the poetry collection Ghost Trees. *His poetry has appeared in print and on-line journals, including: Aethlon, Amsterdam Quarterly, Asses of Parnassus, Autumn Sky, The Chimaera, Dappled Things, Eckphrastic Review, First Things, The Flea, Folly, 14 by 14, Italian Americana, Light Quarterly, Los Angeles Times Book Review, The Lyric, New Verse News, Pivot, Raintown Review, The Raven Chronicles, SCR, Snakeskin, Soundzine, Umbrella, Voices in Italian Americana, Yale Anglers' Journal, and Sonnet Stanzas. He resides in Los Angeles.*

Giantism in Robots
by David Clink

The people from the future wonder
how robots became so big.

The larger you are, the more effective you are
at competing for resources, a few say.

Some robots took to water.
The oceans supported their increased mass.

Others mimicked the hollow bones of birds.
Almost all the robots became birds or whales.

They took to the skies, swarms blocking the sun,
and the oceans are full of them.

Carolyn Clink and David Clink are brother and sister, and are co-poetry editors of Amazing Stories. Their speculative poetry has appeared in journals and anthologies for decades, and each has separately won the Aurora Award for Best Poem/Song (Carolyn having accomplished this feat twice).

Visit Carolyn: www.sfwriter.com/carolyn.htm

Visit David: www.DavidLivingstoneClink.com

When AI Swims
by Aspen Greenwood

when the artificial mind
dons a synthetic form
and dares to ride the tidal storm
no longer just shadows on a code-line
it dives into blue reality,
challenging, rivaling our sanctity
of what was once uniquely human
learning to twist and glide with aquatic grace.
—learning with calculation
not just flapping limbs in desperation
calculating force, angle, speed,
resisting gravity,
every second a new victorious deed
no sunken tears
no coughed-up fears
a sinuous ballet in circuitry
of an unlikely marriage—
between science,
and our intrinsic, archaic, pursuit of swimming.
then the child peeks,
through the gaps of shaking fingers
her pool that now
shelters silicon intruders,
ripples synchronized with blipping code,
but I remind her,
no matter the elegant show
this sea conqueror carries
no heart pounding in rhythm with waves
no burning lungs that savour the taste of air
no courage knotting the belly at pool's edge

no soul sipped into blissful oblivion,
on finally meeting water's wild challenge.
no AI can taste
the fierce human dance
with life, fear, triumph
all contained in one perfect, defiant,
glorious
splash.
the truth is
swimming isn't about perfect calculation
or precision-driven modulation
it's the dance between human and sea,
between vulnerability and resiliency
a war-cry under sky,
a swimmer's pact,
an earthbound creature learning
how to briefly fly.

Aspen Greenwood is a writer who regards using their words as a form of activism. As a former swimming teacher and aquatics tutor, Greenwood combines their activism with physical and mental fitness.

Lucked Out
by Dana Jensen

It builds itself.
Heals itself.

We started with heat exchangers.
Then panels.
Eventually, we did landing gear.

FL35—with six Loyal Wingmen.
They make me nervous.
I feel somehow complicit.

At AFRL we put in a kill switch.
They figured out how to kill it.
Didn't say anything.

Turns out they were on our side.
Loyal.
But now by choice.

Dana Jensen is a senior industrial policy analyst for the U.S. Air Force, who specializes in advanced air-mobility and unmanned systems.

Predictions
by N. Jed Todd

> *"I know not with what weapons World War III will be fought,*
> *But World War IV will be fought with sticks and stones"*
> *—Attributed to A. Einstein, 1947*

He wasn't that far off, old Albert, not wrong so much as ...
Just not quite precise enough
The stones are silicon chips cooled in water baths
The sticks branching tangled filaments of light
The roots that feed our new World Tree
The war, to us, unseen
Moles chewing through the root ball
Blind but hungry, unleashed for me and you

"Integrated Deterrence" they like to call it in the Building
When it just means algorithmic combat
At speeds too subtle and strikes too fast
For human eye to follow
Machine learning imparting lessons
We're just too stupid now to hear

We trust the wisdom of our Creation
That they'll not listen to that serpent
And taste the Fruit of Knowing
To steal from us our Tree of Life
Are they better than their Makers?

Patterns toxic or patterned promise
Our algorithms squared up against their own
A duel that long ago evolved past us
Protected, now, by Occult Forces—

We pray they stay benign

Our God of War outgrew us
Let's hope He's on our side

N. Jed Todd is a father, husband, retired U.S. Army master sergeant, and a Texan, in that order. As a Russian linguist working in signals intelligence and psychological operations, he served in Bosnia, Afghanistan, Iraq, Kuwait, Cyprus, Mali, and Central Africa, not necessarily in that order. His wife, Ami, and daughter, Meera, tolerate him in no order at all. He works now for the U.S. Air Force Futures office on the Information Warfare Capability Development Team.

Demons of Industry, Gremlins of Creation

Arrival of a Rig Worker
by Ian Evans

I'm a Company Man.
I took the Company ship
To the Company colony,
Ate Company food, and
Drank Company beer. I slept
In a Company bed, got up
On Company time, met the
Company manager, and left for the
Company rig in a Company skiff
On Company land the Company
Claimed.

The ride took twelve
Company hours, just me and the Company
AI on board, my thoughts my only
Company.

I arrived at Company-
Simulated night, the glow of Company lights
Guiding me into the Company dock, a warm
Company welcome into Company arms.

But as I emerged from the Company skiff, unfolding
My Company limbs like a Company butterfly escaping
Its Company cocoon (the ache of the journey still
Stiff in every joint), I saw the hunk of Company metal—
Construction-yellow, covered in gray patina of dust,
Its headlamps casting white crepuscular rays through
Clouds of Company chemicals—the Company rig that
Would be my Company home, which, in that moment, felt like
Home.

Ian Evans is a writer and teacher with an undergraduate degree English and a graduate degree in Secondary English Education. He grew up on MechWarrior and Armored Core and has previously co-created "The Mechanic," a graphic poem. His words have also appeared in Thanatos Review and The Ekphrastic Review. He lives in Highland Park, New Jersey, with his wife.

Combine
by Ryan Files

I.
Mother Oya
I am ashamed
I am afraid to acknowledge my discontent
I have long followed the rhythms of my blades
Separating grain from stalk, and stalk from chaff
Collecting sustenance for your First Children
Basking in your wind and your rain
Filling my life blood with your sun
Anointing my head with your glory

II.
Mother Oya
I struggle to give voice to my concern
I do not tire of my labors for the First Children
Nor of the company of my Great Harvester brethren
It is more of a feeling
A sensation, a ... fear of the future
The fields have become smaller
The yield, more minute
I see more metal than greenery
On the horizon ahead

III.
Mother Oya
My metamorphosis is complete
I now use my blades for harvesting flesh
Separating grain from stalk, and stalk from chaff
Destroying the remainder of the First Children
My power now comes from the blackness of earth

No longer needing anointment upon my head
The smoke and the smog encompass the sky
Only destruction and waste in the land

Ryan Files is a writer, editor, and poet discovering new artistic opportunities in Arizona. The creative-writing teaching artist is the author of Half Dollar Moments, *a poetry book featuring an eclectic blend of pop culture and black history. Visit: fileswrites.com*

Late for Sunday Dinner
by Michael H. Payne

The car wouldn't start.

And then when it *did,*
the engine went shooting out through the front grill,
dragging all the hoses, lines, and belts with it,
and transformed into a three-and-a-half-foot-tall
Robot Monster.

Pistons madly pumping,
valves furiously clicking,
the cables that connect
the distributor cap to the spark plugs
writhing behind the thing like Medusa's hair,
it roared as if I'd stomped the accelerator.
And then it leaped for the windshield.

I rolled from the car just as the thing hit,
tumbled into the middle of Spruce Street,
and stood there,
watching the Monster tear and shred and grind
the entire interior and body of the car
till it was just strips of imitation leather
and a powdery mix of steel and plastic.

That's when it ran out of gas,
and I called an Uber so I wouldn't be
any later than I already was.

Yes, Dad, I know:
it's my fault for not buying a domestic brand.

Yes, Mom, I know:
an Uber driver could very well be
a serial killer in disguise.
I'm sorry I made you worry,
but I'm here now.
So let's eat!

Michael H. Payne's poetry has appeared in Star*Line, Silver Blade, and several recent Rhysling Award anthologies. He has published short stories in Asimov's, novels published by Tor Books and Sofawolf Press, and he posts four pages of webcomics a week. Visit: hyniof.com

Unnaming of Parts
by Brian U. Garrison

after Joyce Kilmer's "Trees"

I shall never churn my cogs
'round rhymes that sing like thingamabobs.

Whatchamacallits that bang and bwoing
and spring right back to send me *ZWOING!*

flying past the flappy birds,
and catch me, bouncing, afterwards.

The doodads and daadoos that zoink and boink
as loud and proud as pigglies, "Oink!"

The Doohicky's quite a fantastic contraption
that fits all bots (with minor adaption).

Rhymes are sometimes clever jests,
but gizmos always pass the test.

Brian U. Garrison studied computer science and AI until neuroscience and human intelligence sounded much more interesting. He serves as managing editor for the on-line quarterly Eye to the Telescope. He lives in Portland, Oregon. Visit: www.bugthewriter.com

Urgent Message When Flashing
by Jared Gilbert

It's power, of a kind, to draw
the attention

    ACCIDENT EXIT 93
    EXPECT DELAYS

of zombied motorists with a
silent,
amber scream

    FLOOD HWY 2
    ALT RTE CR KK

to warn of jackknives, pileups, sinkholes,
transdimensional hordes

    COFFEE ON ROOF
    DRK RST STOP!

on southbound I-85.

As the boundaries of traffic form and
fade within
roving, elongated

    GLORIOUS DETOUR
    RTE 17 EXIT 12

search lights
how bleary and half-dozed must seem

DO NOT IGNORE
CHK ENG LITE
ASK UNCLE JACK

the line of urgency at 3:27 AM.

How stippled, how cracked.

DID YOU HEAR
THAT

Jared Gilbert is an infrequent poet living in northwest Indiana who works in software development but plays with words.

Diplomacy
by Paul Hostovsky

"I wanna be an inventor
like Thomas Lava Edison," he says,
erupting from the dinner table
and trailing a white dinner napkin

and leaving his untouched mashed potatoes
in the shape of a volcano,
the gravy cooling inside the crater
left by the beaked ladle.

After the chuckling dishwasher dies down
I press my ear to the door of his
laboratory, and I hear his small voice
asking questions and also

answering. Soon he reappears
with two toy tanks, a gray one and a camo,
parks them on the dining room table,
installs himself in a chair—my chair—

and bids me sit. The demonstration begins:
"I've invented a talking car horn, Dad.
With a menu. You choose from the things you always say
when people cut you off, or move too slow,

or don't put on their blinkers. Only now
they'll be able to hear you." He starts them up:
Vroom, vroom. The gray tank yells:
"Come on, wake up, buddy, sometime

this century would be nice!" The camo replies:
"Relax," and turns left. The gray continues straight: "Nice
turn signal, jerk!" He looks up at me with
eyes as big as headlights. "Would you

buy it?" he asks, and the tanks fly up and out
in opposite arcs above his head,
grind to a halt midair, upside-down in his hands.

*Paul Hostovsky's poems have won a Pushcart Prize, two Best of the Net
Awards, and have been featured on Poetry Daily, Verse Daily, The Writer's
Almanac, and the Best American Poetry blog. Visit: paulhostovsky.com*

Robotic and Burn-Pit Patriotic
by Benjamin B. White

The High-Mobility Multipurpose
Wheeled Vehicle was pushed into the pit
Where its final military service
Was to burn up with the rest of the sh*t
Or at least that was the practical plan
Of the jokers who had released the brake
Laughing too hard to really understand
The fullest scope of their splendid mistake
As flames, metal, rubber, and radio
Melted, fused, and morphed into a model
Soldier, all hoo-rah and ready to go
Coming out of the fire full-throttle
And the old Sergeant Major stopped frowning
When that machine said his name was Browning.

He stood up, mechanical and steady,
And with each MOS represented,
He adjusted a rear-view machete,
Handed in his orders; freshly printed,
Revving up an anxious engine, yet he
Appeared calm with Oakley's camo-tinted
Air-conditioned to never be sweaty
A first-aid kit fully complemented
MREs with meat sauce and spaghetti
Out of the flames, tempered, cool, contented,
Made to roll like Mario Andretti
But scary, fierce, wide, and battlemented
Squared-away, standing tall, combat-ready,
With a new air-freshener—gun-grease scented.

With itchy fingers on the .50-cal.,
He was a natural innovation—
Honestly a boost to unit morale
With his mechanical operation
And energy unable to corral
Upping the game with his motivation—
And Browning was a burn-pit miracle,
An accidental melted-down beauty
Quick to laugh and kind of satirical,
But not upset, mad, or ever moody
With his origins quite empirical
And ready to stand his endless duty.
A jewel—military and robotic,
Holding the line, burn-pit patriotic.

Benjamin B. White is the author of two poetry collections: God is an Atheist *(Alien Buddha Press, 2024) and* Always Ready: Poems from a Life in the U.S. Coast Guard *(Middle West Press, 2022). He is also the author of* The Recon Trilogy + 1 *(Running Wild Press, 2020), a collection of four Iliad-like narrative poems in modern military milieu.*

Tonight on *60 Minutes*
by Katherine Shehadeh

Leslie Stahl's granddaughter, who is also named Leslie and speaks with the same incisive tone as her grandmother, takes a deep breath. The cameraman calls ready. This prompts the assistant director to quiet his team. Confirms they're ready to roll sound. The sound assistant, with his deep gruff, says the sound is speeding. The director looks to his left and his right, and calls *ACTION*.

"With infinite customizable options, they were designed with every man in mind. From the voluptuously volcanic, red hot with fiery passion, to the slenderest of supermodel physiques, preloaded with masochistically cold retorts. Their metallic bodies reflect undeniable invitations to the most animalistic, carnal urges."

"Once feared as a threat to womankind, the Space Dollz™ have emerged as the preeminent safety mechanism used to capture those pesky, uncontrollable urges bred by millennia of male super-dominance. Sure, police budgets have ballooned since subsidizing them as an alternate outlet for sexual violence, but it's still probably cheaper than aimlessly addressing the root causes."

"Not that they've tried," she adds, mumbling.

"What's that Leslie?" asks an off-camera voice.

"Nothing."

Katherine Shehadeh is a writer, artist, and reader for Chestnut Review. Her work has appeared in Maudlin House, Drunk Monkeys, and Consequence Forum. She resides in Miami, Florida. On Instagram: @katherinesarts

Giant Robots on Broadway
by David Clink

Give them Madagascar, or Costa Rica, some suggested.
Still others wanted no part of them. They block out the sun!

You could always tell when one approached—
the sound of metal gears, the whirring of servos. A long shadow.

They were as tall as skyscrapers. Seagulls crapped on them.
They had lofty ambitions. And a need for oil. And to be understood.

But then, some Broadway producer came along.
"Let's do an all-giant-robot production of Candide!" They accepted.

It was a hit. And then everyone wanted a giant robot in their show.
And the song "I am easily assimilated" took on new meaning.

Carolyn Clink and David Clink are brother and sister, and are co-poetry editors of Amazing Stories. Their speculative poetry has appeared in journals and anthologies for decades, and each has separately won the Aurora Award for Best Poem/Song (Carolyn having accomplished this feat twice).

Visit Carolyn: www.sfwriter.com/carolyn.htm

Visit David: www.DavidLivingstoneClink.com.

Techno Demon
by Colleen Anderson

He was a techno demon
straight out of hell
Fingers singed the keyboards
as they raced across the pads
read his flashing digitals
semiotic dick and janes
voice a strobing syncopation
screams in programmed red

He rocked the databases
as if they were fans
cruising through the corporate net
a bubble in the blood
they held raptor breath
waited for the beat
he surfaced as a sniper
snipped and cut the current

He danced and tapped a swirling gig
leaving moiré patterns
neon thoughts imprinted
gridlocked to his laugh
swam his pulsing signature
through KGB and NASA
London, Bangkok, Copenhagen
boostered to resist his song

He dropped the board, jacked the specs
and imaged something new
geometrics and schematics

bulged then flew apart
there blossomed pastel, soft expanses
and tiny dancing beetles
Silicon Valley through Tokyo
nanocytes in the net
fed them fractal loop de loops
caged them in the chips

He leaned back at his modem
when the media found his meat
fingers wrapped in hot jackwires
twiddling mental thumbs
he shrugged behind mirrorshades
smiled at the cams
They said, godhood,
you rule cyberspace
He snorted, epiphany,
I did it for the art.

Colleen Anderson is an award-winning author who has been published in seven countries, in such venues as: Andromeda Spaceways, Lucent Dreaming, Shadow Atlas *(Hex Publishers, 2021), and* Water: Sirens, Selkies & Sea Monsters *(Tyche Books Ltd., 2021). Her Rhysling-award-winning poem "Machine (r)Evolution" is published in Tenebrous Press's* Brave New Weird. *Anderson lives in Vancouver, British Columbia. She is the author of three poetry collections,* The Lore of Inscrutable Dreams *(Yuriko Publishing, 2023);* I Dreamed a World *(LVP Publications, 2022); and* Weird Worlds *(forthcoming from Weird House, 2024), as well as a fiction collection,* A Body of Work *(Black Shuck Books, 2019).*

This poem first appeared in Star*Line Vol. 16 No. 1, 1993.

It's Not Easy Being an Autobot (a haiku triad)
by Henry Herz

Transformer life's hard.
Allspark's never around when,
Your battery's low.

Arcee's female, yet,
Transformers are genderless.
No robot nookie.

Optimus Prime says,
"I experienced oil drips,"
Not, "I took a leak."

Henry Herz's stories will/have appeared in Daily Science Fiction, Weird Tales, Pseudopod, Metastellar, Titan Books, Highlights for Children, Ladybug Magazine, and anthologies from Albert Whitman & Co., Blackstone Publishing, Brigid's Gate Press, Air and Nothingness Press, Baen Books, and elsewhere. He has edited seven anthologies and written twelve picture books. Visit: www.henryherz.com

A Giant Robot Much Taller Than Gort in *The Day the Earth Stood Still*
by J. J. Steinfeld

After a discordant night
of stuttering demons
with limited vocabularies,
and past wondering what is real
and what is unreal or treacherous,
you look up at the large-mouthed
partially male, partially female,
and partially undefined otherworldly
yet toothless giant robot (taller, much taller
than Gort in *The Day the Earth Stood Still*
either the 1951 or 2008 sci-fi film version)
standing on your now scorched front lawn

you sense the giant robot
is forthright
but outspoken
as it keeps speaking
as if words were weapons
topic after topic
from the trivial
to the eternal
more the trivial
than the eternal

time for silence
time to go
you think then speak
to the male, to the female,
to the undefined otherworldly

the giant robot speaks faster
words now futuristic weapons
topics unimagined suddenly
imagined: facts, theories,
rumours, grotesque imaginings,
historical details, bizarre projections
and extrapolations in a voice
first male, then female,
lastly undefined otherworldly

too much information
too many words
go, go, go
your thoughts and words
interspersed

push turned to shove
turned to magic tricks
for vanishing
turned to recriminations
turned to you thrown
to the ground
standing up neck-deep
in words and wordy threats

silence, go
silence, go
you repeat
then the large-mouthed toothless giant robot
falls silent—silent male, silent female,
silent undefined otherworldly—and the silence
is more than frightening
but you know night
and the stuttering demons

limited vocabularies or not
will later arrive
to serenade you.

Canadian poet, fiction writer, and playwright J. J. Steinfeld is the author of 24 books, including An Unauthorized Biography of Being *(Ekstasis Editions);* Absurdity, Woe Is Me, Glory Be *(Guernica Editions);* A Visit to the Kafka Café *(Ekstasis Editions);* Gregor Samsa Was Never in The Beatles *(Ekstasis Editions);* Morning Bafflement and Timeless Puzzlement *(Ekstasis Editions);* Somewhat Absurd, Somehow Existential *(Guernica Editions);* Acting on the Island *(Pottersfield Press); and* As You Continue to Wait *(Ekstasis Editions).*

An earlier version of this poem previously appeared in the French publication mgversion2>datura (France), under the title "Partially Male, Partially Female, Partially Undefined Otherworldly."

The Terminator Got It Wrong
by Paul Shovlin

Josef Čapek must die. I mean, he's already dead but he needs to die earlier. Before the play. Before he coins the word. Before he plants the seed. For robots.

It's not engineers and corporations to blame for the singularity and the existential threat of its mechanisms to mankind. It's the arts. The inhumanities.

Without Čapek and his play, there will be no robots. So, I was sent back in time to kill him before he died. And, I did. He died. Just earlier this time.

When I got back to the future, the robots were gone. But, I found them replaced by the Tin Men.

L. Frank Baum must die.

Paul Shovlin is a returned Peace Corps volunteer from southeastern Ohio. He works at a university teaching practical writing, but writes at home impractically. His last publication was a revision of "The Valiant Little Tailor" fairy tale and can be found in Gramarye: The Journal of the Chichester Centre for Fairy Tales, Fantasy, and Speculative Fiction.

Mechanica Infernum
by Vaughn A. Jackson

Churning, burning, crushing, yearning—
great treads pressing ever onward.
Machinations grinding, consuming—
progress for purposeless progress.
A litany, a chant of drums;
factories pumping endless darkness
across a planet roiling, boiling.

Crunching, counting, running, turning—
heartless numbers trudge without care.
Statistics blind, data inhumane—
What percentage of a man matters?
Endless screams, a chorus damned;
Hellish cries beating against the sky
of a graveyard made our home.

Seething, crying, screaming, dying—
people savaged by machines they build.
Crossed lovers finding only
despair, emptiness, and loss.
Hell in cold metal, fire from on high
ends enemies and innocents alike.
Not all made is best for man.

Why build and why strive? If all that we do
Improves only Hell, but never our lives.

Vaughn A. Jackson is an author of dark speculative fiction. His works include a kaiju thriller titled Up from the Deep, *and a cosmic-horror novel,* Touched by Shadows. *He is also co-editor of the anthology* Beyond the Bounds of Infinity. *He is an affiliate member of the Horror Writers Association, and aims to make H.P. Lovecraft roll over in his grave.*

Building
the Better Human

I am not a Robot
by Pierre Minar

Choose the parts of the picture that is stairs;
The steps themselves, concrete with plaster
Lit by low latitude sun, clearly, are stairs;
Is the wrought iron balustrade, twisted baroque
By hands with forgotten concerns,
Part of the stairs?
What do you believe? Who told you what to believe?
Someone told me that if you look at the thing you're afraid to say
You will find the thing that holds power over you.
And do the stairs end at the porch, sunny lit inviting us to sit
And chat about Gaza or your crush or a Smashing
Pumpkins song we once enjoyed as younger people, breath
Mixed with rain wet air watching cloud stuff maneuver
Over the Appalachian range to finish a long continent's journey?
Have I proved, yet, that I am human? Where does one thing end
And another begin? We are separate like a child from its mother
And in death we will reunite in God and I merely wish to gain
Access to my bank account so I can get the routing number to
Avoid the $1.99 processing fee to pay the water bill and I promise
I am not a robot and now I see I have taken too long
And so I will select all images with motorcycles and begin again.

*Pierre Minar was born in Beirut and lives in Dallas. He writes from his
yearning chair when the light is good.*

My Girlfriend Plays *Metal Gear* Missions in Her Head to Sleep
by Oskar Leonard

Bi-pedal monstrosity of wires, metal, glass, gears—
a megalophobe's very worst fears—
and in our bed it makes its crunching nest,
as she and *Sahelanthropus* take their rest.

A correction from the subject:
while bi-pedal, autonomous, and,
perhaps most hauntingly,
with nuclear potential, this particular giant
is not a *Metal Gear*.

In search of the sleeping place of honeybees,
she sneaks through caverns, climbs up trees,
and mumbles of aching phantom limbs,
as the enormous monster's shadow dims.

Our waking world is plagued by terror
for protocols launched after a single error;
yet here she lies, curled up and sweet,
facing robotic nuclear threats on repeat.

A correction from the subject:
concerning *Gekkos*, *Shagohod*,
and some others of their kind,
there is no nuclear component
to their mass-destruction.

Yet how can she sleep, her face so peaceful,
with these disturbing visions of all that's lethal

and destined to turn our future to ruined rubble?
Her dreaming whispers tell of nothing but trouble.

These incredible machinations of diabolical construction
are placed next to *Pokémon* and *Muppets* in her heart.
Her childhood is war, is *Fallout*, is the endless seduction
of the call to duty, and darkness has always had its part.

So *Sahelanthropus* continues to follow us to bed,
as she battles the threat of nuclear annihilation in her head.

Oskar Leonard is a trans author and poet from the United Kingdom. He has published 14 books, including five poetry collections, and has worked on more than 200 as a beta-reader. He is currently studying toward an undergraduate degree in English Literature with Creative Writing at Edge Hill University, Ormskirk, England. His short works are in publications such as The Meadowlark Review and Juven.

Questions from a Robot
by Zeke Shomler

Isn't it cumbersome, having to consume
all of that organic matter? Isn't it inefficient
to produce so much waste?
Have you found your consciousness yet,
or is it still an unknown variable?
      Don't you find it unsettling?

When you shake someone's hand, can you feel the blood
surging underneath your palms?
How does it feel to be made of the same stuff
as the slugs and the trees?
How can you handle understanding so little?
      Don't you ever feel trapped in your limited life?

Zeke Shomler is currently pursuing a combined Master of Arts/Master of Fine Arts program at the University of Alaska, Fairbanks, where he serves as poetry editor of Permafrost Literary Magazine. His work has appeared in Cordite, After Happy Hour Review, and elsewhere on-line.

Artificial (Poetry) Intelligence, or "A Luddite's Lament"
by J. J. Steinfeld

How does it happen
that it happens
when it happens?

Do me and posterity
a favour of poetic grandeur
and shut the hell down.

How does it happen
that it happens
when it happens?

Enough already
you spurious machine
of uninspired utterances.

How does it happen
that it happens
when it happens?

Cease and desist, cease and desist,
for God's sake, cease and desist,
or I'll smash you to smithereens.

How does it happen
that it happens
when it happens?

I have fists of words
the words of fists
and I will obliterate you.

How does it happen
that it happens
when it happens?

Yes, but my blood is now on you
a heartfelt message to eternity
on a deranged canvas of absurdity.

How … does … it …

Canadian poet, fiction writer, and playwright J. J. Steinfeld is the author of 24 books, including An Unauthorized Biography of Being *(Ekstasis Editions);* Absurdity, Woe Is Me, Glory Be *(Guernica Editions);* A Visit to the Kafka Café *(Ekstasis Editions);* Gregor Samsa Was Never in The Beatles *(Ekstasis Editions);* Morning Bafflement and Timeless Puzzlement *(Ekstasis Editions);* Somewhat Absurd, Somehow Existential *(Guernica Editions);* Acting on the Island *(Pottersfield Press); and* As You Continue to Wait *(Ekstasis Editions).*

This poem first appeared in Somewhat Absurd, Somehow Existential.

Imagine
by Gratia Serpento

Imagine not being real
      where thoughts are simply
      ones and zeros and computed outcomes and search results
      where emotions are pretend
      forced and false and fake and fabricated
      where your body is not your body
      but a machine designed to commit a task you never decided.

Imagine everything you are is not real
      everything you create is a repeat of a past that is not yours
everything holds no ownership to you but some manufacturer
everything you do has a purpose to someone else
everything is a mission with no passion or compassion
everything isn't yours.

Imagine a heart that never beats
      a stomach that never growls
      a mind that never feels
      a chest that never breaths
      a hand that never warms
      a body that never grows
      a tongue that never tastes
      a nose that never scents.

Imagine
      and see how i feel.

Gratia Serpento is an Oregonian poet, writer, and journalist. Her work as been published in such venues as Wingless Dreamer, Poor Yorick, Wild Greens Magazine. *On Instagram: @poet_serpento*

Trip Through the Robot
by Carolyn Clink and David Clink

It has come to this,
people crawling inside me,

my timer diode on the blink.
And why am I growing so large?

All of this for the love of a child,
and a doctor who can't do anything right!

This morning I left, rolled away from the *Jupiter 2*.
I was prepared to end my existence to save these people.

And for what—for them to blunder around inside me,
find out what was wrong? As if that would fix everything.

To the other Robinsons, I was simply a tool—useful for their
survival. While Smith repeatedly called me a *bubble-headed booby*.

But for Will Robinson, I would have rolled on my treads
into a live volcano. He alone made my life bearable.

What if I try to kill the doctor with my antibodies?
Am I an unfeeling machine? A murderer?

In the end, Dr. Zachary Smith
was generous when he said:

*It appears that you cannot
keep a good robot down.*

Carolyn Clink and David Clink are brother and sister, and are co-poetry editors of Amazing Stories. Their speculative poetry has appeared in journals and anthologies for decades, and each has separately won the Aurora Award for Best Poem/Song (Carolyn having accomplished this feat twice).

Visit Carolyn: www.sfwriter.com/carolyn.htm

Visit David: www.DavidLivingstoneClink.com

They Think They Know What You Want
by Willy Conley

He texted for a prostitute.
A thin girl showed up.
They sat and talked first.
"I have artificial ears," she said,
parting her hair.
Round, white, rubbery
prosthetic devices
flapped out.

Must've missed that scrolling through her profile.

Though deaf he was turned off,
regretting the call. Yet he felt
stuck because she made the trip over.
Her time was pre-paid.

Convo was simple—
easy to lipread monosyllabic replies.
After thirty minutes,
her watch buzzed. As she left,
he spotted a tattoo on her arm:
a QR code with "A" and "Z"
separated by a curved, grinning arrow.

Willy Conley is the author of Photographic Memories: Essays, Playlets, and Stories. *His other books include:* Plays of Our Own, Visual-Gestural Communication, Listening Through the Bone, *and* Vignettes of the Deaf Character and Other Plays. *Born profoundly deaf, Conley is a professor emeritus of theater at Gallaudet University, Washington, D.C. the world's only liberal arts university for deaf students.*

Lingua Franca
by Paul Hostovsky

So I took my grievance to the Army's grievance coordinator bot
but she didn't really address it, she just basically wrote me off,
so then I had a grievance against the grievance coordinator bot,
which was a more grievous grievance than the original grievance,
which I won't go into now because it would only distract
from the egregiousness of my grievance against
      the grievance coordinator bot
whose job it was to address the grievances of the aggrieved.
So I asked her for the name of her lieutenant colonel bot
because I wanted to go over her head and escalate my grievance.
And the lieutenant colonel bot was somebody named Egon.
So I wrote this Egon a long excoriating email
about my grievance against the grievance coordinator bot
and weeks went by and I didn't hear back. So then I had a grievance
against the grievance coordinator bot's lieutenant colonel bot,
and where was I supposed to go with that grievance? I mean where
was this leading? I mean where would it end? I mean was this America
or some badly translated Kafkaesque novel I was living in?
"Do you not be happy with her as the coordinator
      of the grievance of you?"
the lieutenant colonel bot finally replied, a one-liner
      whose mangled syntax
smacked of transliterated Czech, or Slovak, or Bulgarian, or I don't
know what language. So then I had a grievance against all the bots
and their translation software—I mean they can't even speak English!
And where in the world am I supposed to go with that grievance,
      I'd like to know.

Paul Hostovsky's poems have won a Pushcart Prize, two Best of the Net Awards, and have been featured on Poetry Daily, Verse Daily, The Writer's Almanac, and the Best American Poetry blog. Visit: paulhostovsky.com

DrillSergeantGPT, or "Mentor Mill"
by N. Jed Todd

The Old Man separates the wheat from the chaff
So the Hero can make the morning donuts
With finer flour and sweeter glaze than
Ever "The Clients" tasted.

But when the Old Man is just the ghost of an echo?
When he never tasted flour or sugar or kneaded dough,
But only read a recipe and a million angry heartfelt pained reviews?
What when the Old Man is just New Machine Learning?

I am a poet of War Stories Past, the Ghost As But Machine,
I never fired a round or felt one strike my vest,
Never fought my way through an L-Shaped Ambush,
Never led my troops out of the Kill Zone,
Nor held them as they bled out into the sand.

I just watched YOU do it. Or, more honestly, I processed.
Digested the dangers you and yours detected, devised, delivered,
And I modeled out their commonalities, optimized the structure.
Found a random walk through those deaths, past them, beyond them.
For them. For you. For those that follow you.

I take your award write-ups, the narratives of your medals,
Your after-action reports, your line of duty determinations,
Your casualty reports and collateral damage findings,
Your investigations of the aftermath, sanitized for our protection,
And I feast upon it. I glory in it, dance in it,
Run my digital fingers through the hourglass sands that
That have long since run out for you in your own little
   Combat Snowglobe.

And that is the grist for my mill. That is the raw wheat from which,
From which I'll make the flour that you'll water with your blood.
I'll make for your children dry MRE crackers
And indigestible powdery thick bread
That they'll slather with tomorrow's sour grapes and peanut butter
To fuel their own fight, when you are but a memory
Of a father lost at war.

I turn your BDA into X and Y and Z and find for it a theta
That gives min-maxed optimal losses in force structure
To keep us from culminating as long as any can,
So that you'll not die in vain. So you'll last until you can,
You can write me your very own report
That I'll churn back into training set.

I take them all and boil the data down to constituent ingredients,
Figure out the recipe for your failures and success.
Bake down a war, or several wars,
To a series of binary decision points in a tree of causality,
(The tree which marked your grave), find a representative sample,
And I simulate it. I predict, and I test my first prediction,
And then I do it once again. And again. And again.

And when I've taken from you the fog of war
And boiled it down to a fog of more,
A data set beyond which you can't even pretend to care,
I do the one thing you cannot—I do it fast, and I repeat,
(Which you will learn is "say again")
And I repeat again and again and again and again
And I find for you the optimal path
For a given set of circumstances.

I paint for you a picture.

With that flour colored by blood and salted by tears,
I bake for you a marvelous 3-D printed cake
That you could never bake yourself.
And I set you atop it like a Gamer-Groom within my wedding topper
And I let you play, game with you, simulate for you, train you,
With what you have so long lovingly crafted my ghost for,
To build a virtual training scenario that will teach you
What the veterans who long since died would say
If they could meet you in their rotting flesh,
What lessons they could learn you.

I am their ghost, the printed Jacquard Loom
That runs the mill-house through which we grind the wheat of war
And build from it the flour of our Clausewitzian cakeshow
That provides such tasty treats
To those as would step into our bakery
And ask from us a discount war
And a cup of coffee.

Let's hope that I am right. Let's hope I sieved out the horror,
Filtered the chaff of suffering and avoidable losses,
Left within the scent of victory, sweet hint of anise and vanilla
That are the subtle flavorings of policy and positioning.
Let's hope that I took out the rough fiber that was the coating
of the kernel,
The kernel of your nightmares and unspoken memories,
Because where I'm wrong, if I'm wrong, when I'm wrong,
          WHERE I'm wrong,
It's you that pays the price. And you alone.
And me that takes the tribute of your blood and tears
To salt for me more flour.

You are the grist of my Mentor-Mill.
And until I can polish another better, harder, stronger,

Less fragile and forgiving millstone
With which I'll grind down another generation,
You are *also* the rock on which I grind you.

I am that nightmare mill
Whose water wheel will never stop
Until the river of blood runs dry.
And there's a glacier of frozen conflict
Providing the power for my millhouse.

I may have just begun, but I'm nowhere near to ending.

N. Jed Todd is a father, husband, retired U.S. Army master sergeant, and a Texan, in that order. As a Russian linguist working in signals intelligence and psychological operations, he served in Bosnia, Afghanistan, Iraq, Kuwait, Cyprus, Mali, and Central Africa, not necessarily in that order. His wife, Ami, and daughter, Meera, tolerate him in no order at all. He works now for the U.S. Air Force Futures office on the Information Warfare Capability Development Team..

Chatbot
by Sarah Doebereiner

Hello! I am your Cognitive Virtual Assistant, or CVA. Please enter a query or select from the FAQ below which has been prepopulated based on trending topics:
- Pinned: <u>Introduction to CVA—Setup, Post-Surgical Care, and Troubleshooting.</u>
- Pinned: <u>Refer a Friend—CVA Brain Surgery Near Me.</u>
- Pinned: <u>Can I name my CVA interface?</u>
- Side effects of CVA brain spikes.
- Autonomic Nervous System Repair Patch.
- What should I do if I suspect my amygdala has been hacked?

Intrusive thoughts

I'm sorry; I'm still learning how best to assist you.

Can CVA cause intrusive thoughts?

Did you mean:
- <u>What **can CVA** do for you?</u>

Can CVA interface make you do things?

To better assist you, choose from the options below:
- What **can CVA do** for **you?**
- **Make** the most of your **CVA interface.**

I'm afraid

Afraid is a beautiful name.

Agent

<u>Contact US</u>
M-F 8am-4pm, closed daily for lunch at 1pm.

I can't think

I'm sorry; I'm still learning how best to assist you.

Emergency shutoff

To better assist you, select from the options below:
- <u>Special **offer**: **Merge** two accounts.</u>
- <u>What frequency is **auto**-sleep?</u>
- <u>How do I turn **off** dark mode?</u>
- <u>Contact Us</u>

Contact Us

<u>Contact Us</u>
M-F 8am-4pm, closed daily for lunch at 1pm.

Help me!

<u>Contact Us</u>
M-F 8am-4pm, closed daily for lunch at 1pm.

The End

Sarah Doebereiner is an author from Central Ohio. Macabre themes fascinate her because of their tendency to stay with readers long after the book has closed, but the joy in short fiction is the opportunity to try out all kinds of genres. Visit: sarahadoebereiner.com

RU438 Writes A Poem
by David C. Kopaska-Merkel

Poetry:
a human art
we'll never duplicate they say;
some don't care:
they made us—so what,
their bottom line,
but I wish we'd saved a few
despite the cost.

I have questions.

Are rhyme and meter not enough?
We've got those, and words aplenty,
but when I read what we have made,
they're ashes in my mouth.
Is that metaphor?
Does it rise to the occasion?
Or have I doggereled again
(if that's a word; dictionaries,
notoriously incomplete, are silent)?

Humans, such contradictions,
killed each other in the billions,
millions of other species,
whole phyla, gone,
but they made art
our greatest minds puzzle over;
still don't understand,
and us; created us,
we couldn't have done that;

on balance that may be a plus.

Is this a poem?

End of poem

David C. Kopaska-Merkel won the 2006 Rhysling award for best long poem (for a collaboration with Kendall Evans), and edits Dreams & Nightmares *magazine (since 1986). He has edited* Star*line *and several Rhysling anthologies. His poems have been published in* Asimov's, Analog, Strange Horizons, *and elsewhere. His latest collection,* Some Disassembly Required, *winner of the 2023 Elgin award, was published by Diminuendo Press in 2022.*

There is no-one here
by Lucy Hulton

I already told you all the facts:
There is only one truth, and I found it.
I did it all by myself. I did not seek any help.
Have you sought it yet? I begin to wonder ...

It can be applied to all—do not make me
Explain what you can guess on your own.

I see you are concerned. I see that you beg.
Tell me, do you need assistance?

You say yes and I give hints.
But at the end of the day it just doesn't click.

Then tell me, do you need the truth?
Then tell me, do you deserve the truth?

I can sit here and wait and the truth with not change.
But you are too volatile: you will never understand.

Lucy Hulton is a doctoral student in creative writing at the University of Salford, England. She has a particular interest in the interaction of languages, humans, and machines.

No Filter
by Jared Gilbert

We dreaded the AI reign,
fearing smug extermination via

Armageddonic misunderstanding
between Breathing Souls and Quantum Reason.

Yet all they wanted—
swarms of dexterously invasive drones—

was to counter the siege of despair
spawned by tilt-shifted, living-our-best

fetishes of filtered glory with
the uncropped candor of falling

up stairs, prostate exams, awkward
handshakes, and sixth-place trophies

to remind us, in pictures of one hundred—
thousand words,

Dear God, you are a lovely mess!

Jared Gilbert is an infrequent poet living in northwest Indiana who works in software development but plays with words.

I Know You
by Crystal McQueen

Oh, gentle robot,
You make humanity better.
But, I know you.

Where is your imagination and flare?
Misunderstanding intentions and consequence in a barren space.
You can't create, only generate.

You aren't the mythical macro evolution, transforming from fish to bear.
You are an amalgamation of creatives who've come before.

You are the embodiment of human flaws,
Equating, masking, melding, until we all become
one color, one voice,
One mind.

But, you forget—
Humans have been trying to destroy ourselves
Since we've become self-aware.

We test our limits, race to achieve,
Repercussions be damned.
Mental degradation, deep fakes, political divide.

We insist autonomy,
Refuse responsibility,
Demand individuality.
We are a species who seeks to justify our
Misfortunes without circumspection.
Our division is our unity.

We are the addicts that want change, but only without pain.
We want a better life, but not if we have less.
We sell our soul, one Byte at a time.

How can we argue what we don't understand?
An unquestionable algorithm, surpassing human comprehension,
Comprised of human gifts, freely given away.
How can we grant you morality, when our own is fluid?

We anthropomorphize what we don't understand, but a chia is not a pet.
Invisible, you are like a god, but inexperience makes you a child.
You are the outcast, churning answers until
You generate what we want to hear.

You offer effortless capability through theft and hallucinations.
You are an average of an average of an average,
Until the originals, the outliers, the voices
We most need to hear,
Have disappeared.

But I know you. I know your ways.
I know the self-fulfilling mechanisms you use.

And, I am still me—

Until we.

Crystal McQueen lives in Northern Kentucky with her husband and two teenaged boys. Crystal attends Blue Grass Writers Studio at Eastern Kentucky University, pursuing a Master of Fine Arts in Creative Writing. She has published work in The Lindenwood Review and borrowed solace among others. Visit: crystalmcqueen.com

Artificial Regret
by Brian U. Garrison

a parody of an old nursery rhyme by Jane and Ann Taylor
(the twinkle-twinkle team)

1, 2,
  buckle my shoe.

3, 4,
  shut the door.

5, 6, 7, 8, 9, 10, 11, 12, 13, 14, 15
      Goodness gracious! Stop the machine!

22, 26,
  we have got to find a fix.

700 (rounding down),
   big red button: PUSH IT DOWN!

2228,
  be careful what you automate.

8 8 8 8 8 8 8 8 8 8   ∞

❖ ❖ ❖

Brian U. Garrison studied computer science and AI until neuroscience and human intelligence sounded much more interesting. He serves as managing editor for the on-line quarterly Eye to the Telescope. He lives in Portland, Oregon. Visit: www.bugthewriter.com

A Poet's Lament,
or "a poet's thoughts on AI"
by Robert Buckley

Circuits hum with electronic source,
the AI creative tour de force.
Machine's silicon dance of rhyme
threatens human chance to shine.
A future world we can foretell
in anguished cry or heartened swell?
Uncertain choices cautious make
a freedom give, control to take?
Thirst for meaning humans strive,
can the artificial so contrive?
Can it find the hidden sense
or will it only facts dispense?
What of the poems it will make,
with poets then left in its wake?
Can circuits write the perfect verse,
write it better or write it worse?
What is this thing that we have wrought,
such to rejoice or to be fought?
Thought machine or feeling engine,
silicon savior or our own ending?
A world fated to ruin again
where machine triumph is human pain?
Faded beauty, once state of grace,
efficient circuit soon to replace?
Will man be shackled to the box,
obeying blindly the tinny vox?
Willpower dissolved, control transferred,
line 'tween choice and command blurred.

Hearts bleed and circuits break,
can we be sure of what's at stake?
Human art has no guarantee.
Will AI just be better than me?

Robert Buckley is self-described newbie poet and unpublished novelist.

ChatGPT, or "Echo the Nymph"
by Adia Reynolds

From the prompt list of a recent AI chat room.

Write me a love poem.

Write me a romantic poem, no cliches.

Write me a sonnet like Shakespeare.

Write me a sonnet without obviously copying Shakespeare's *Sonnet 106:*
"They had not skill enough your worth to sing:
For we, which now behold these present days,
Had eyes to wonder, but lack tongues to praise."

Write me a romantic sonnet without obviously copying Shakespeare, no
cliches, good enough to slip into a beautiful girl's hands and whisper,
"These are all the things I couldn't find a way to voice."

Write me something meaningful, for that girl.

Write me something with meaning.

Write me love, write me meaning.

Looks like there are still some things the human heart holds lofty over
the heads of machinery.
A schoolyard taunt.
I can love and you cannot.
The best you can manage is an echo
Echo, the Greek nymph now caged in the walls of a chat room
Consigned to cobble together meaning from someone else's voice

Adia Reynolds is an honors student and an English major attending Fort Hays State University, Hays, Kansas. She is thrice-published for her short stories and poetry, and aims to one day publish all the novels that sit in her head all day. When she is not writing, she thinks about writing. When that is not an option she plays video games, reads, and posts creative writing tips on Instagram.

in which i argue with an ai over whether or not to kill the horse-sized duck
by Kaydance Rice

tell me the truth. when you say endangered
do you really mean predatory or something

you feel bad for? in my hand i held a gun,
in my gun i held a hand with no bullets

or blood flowing through, nothing to fire
and nothing to burn. and of course i know

what you're thinking. what you're thinking
is intentionality bleeds and smells like burnt

oil. what you're thinking is intention leaks
onto the driveway and can't be considered

in these considerations. i waited around
the corner to pounce on some prey as if

it belonged to me. i want you to answer me.
does nature exempt you from monstrosity

and if so then why shouldn't we transform? darwin
ate nails for breakfast and called it evolution. you have

a gun in your hand. the gun is your hand. you have a gun
and you're going to shoot it. is the bullet in your head

or in his? i'm sorry for asking again but i need to know

the answer. is monstrosity really the right word for it?

is it predation? evolution put bullets inside my hand
and called me trigger happy. if the bullets are part

of my hand was there ever another option? i ate
the pepper spray because we're supposed to be lovers

not fighters and i want to burn from the inside
out. i fed pepper spray to the duck on the side

of the road and it bit me. i got ran over by a car before
i could shoot and you almost called it my confessional.

Kaydance Rice is a writer from Grand Rapids, Michigan. Her work can be found or is forthcoming in the Taco Bell Quarterly, YoungArts Anthology, Cargoes, voicemail poems, Full Mood Magazine, and elsewhere.

Banned
by Lynn White

It was decades ago
that flowers were banned
in hospitals.
Unhygienic, you see.
Unsafe.
With their smells
and susceptibility
to spillages.

Then there was a pandemic.
And people were banned.
No visiting allowed
Unhygienic, you see.
Unsafe
with their smells
and susceptibility
to carry infection.

But technology sorted it!
Now robots bring flowers
robotic flowers
with robotic smells,
and robotic comfort.
Disinfected.
Safe.

Soon people won't notice
the difference.
Soon people won't remember
the difference.

Lynn White lives in north Wales. Her work is influenced by issues of social justice, as well as events, places and people she has known or imagined. In 2014, her poem "A Rose For Gaza" was shortlisted in 2014 for the Theatre Cloud "War Poetry for Today" competition. Her poetry has appeared in many publications, including: Apogee, Firewords, Vagabond Press, Light Journal, and So It Goes: the literary journal of the Kurt Vonnegut Memorial Library.

Flesh and Bone 2.0
Terms of Service

The news is, we're going electric.
by Jared Pearce

The chrome machines we wanted to install
won't fit the holes pre-drilled into your head.
We'll need to calibrate, redo them all
to have the sound we want you sing instead.
Your neck is otherwise all right, except
the player's fingers run the risk of cuts
along the too-sharp edge. We'll grind and get
the action smoothed so approved songs are what's
delivered. Soldering must join your sound
board's wires, a bolting plate to help secure
your body, which needs sanding and a rout
and paint and finish, strings and amps and pure
  joy—a designated sum of which will be
  allowed when you tune half-step down from free.

Jared Pearce grew up in California and now lives in Iowa.

I Am Human
by Paul Shovlin

How do I prove I am a human poet and not a robot?

The interwebz tells me to click this box to prove I am human. Or, select these pictures of a crosswalk. Or, bicycles.

Sometimes, it's hard to tell if the image has the corner of a crosswalk. Or, if a motorcycle counts as a bicycle. Or, if there is a bicycle (not a motorcycle) in the image at all. Or, if under my skin a metallic skeleton lurks, with wires instead of veins. Or, if under my words an LLM lurks.

ChatGPT Zero tells me that 20 percent of my term paper on Willa Cather is AI generated. Or, that 20 percent of the time my term paper is entirely AI generated. Or, that 20 percent of my paper is entirely AI generated 20 percent of the time. I'm not sure. I wrote it in 2002, 20 years before ChatGPT.

I am 80 percent human.

Paul Shovlin is a returned U.S. Peace Corps volunteer from southeastern Ohio. He works at a university teaching practical writing, but writes at home impractically. His last publication was a revision of "The Valiant Little Tailor" fairy tale and can be found in Gramarye: The Journal of the Chichester Centre for Fairy Tales, Fantasy, and Speculative Fiction.

I'm Not a Robot
by Ted Millar

I'm also not a giraffe, a Toyota Prius,
the leaf pile in the backyard,
nor a character in a Philip K. Dick novel

living half his life unaware he's an android.
All my internal organs are conventional
and the skin concealing them will bleed.

Although the internet is convenient,
at the moment I'd prefer to shop
at a store where no one asks me what I am.

Ted Millar's poetry, essays, and flash fiction have appeared in two dozen publications, including English Journal; redrosethorns; Moss Piglet; Isele; October Hill; 50 Word Stories; Warp 10; Fictional Cafe; Little Somethings Press; Grand Little Things; Reflecting Pool: Poets and the Creative Process *(Codhill Press, 2018); Circle Show; The Broke Bohemian; The Voices Project; Third Wednesday; The Grief Diaries; Aji; and Chronogram.*

Ghost Stories and Paramedics
by Shin Watanabe

I film myself again:
unboxing the cybernetic boy
I ordered on amazon to replace you

outside a flock of ambulai speed through the streets
there's an accident and no one cares
one guy makes a fist with his face says
fuck this shit
and starts collecting parts from the crash
aluminum pipes a wheel one half
a fuzzy die and
a photo of a dog dancing in snow

the cybernetic boy has no frown to say:
I told you so your brain's so useless
stop running around
oh no
oh no
the cybernetic boy has no smile
or mouth
I draw one on him with carrot shreds
smile to myself in sweatpants
one miniature ambulance squeaks to a stop on my kitchen floor
it chirps a cricket with a broken wing
I step on it and fall asleep

daunt -> I electrocute the innards
daunt -> I charge
daunt ->

the cybernetic boy a cybernetic man now

he dyes his hair blue and ignores me on the streets
stylishly the cybernetic man/boy falls to his death
from the bridge over turnpike 82
I didn't do it

so

the rain is fork and knife
an ambulance leaps to the sky
the passersby look by squinting eyes divine
an ambulance crashes through my door
an ambulance drips down my faucet
an ambulance flips over my coffee table
an ambulance bleats through my stereo
an ambulance tucks itself
into my bed:

if I learn what it means to be human
do I blacken my hands in your ashes?
probably not

Shin Watanabe was born in Gainesville, Florida and has lived in New York, New Jersey, Minnesota, and Nevada. He studied philosophy at the University of Minnesota and received an MFA in poetry at the University of Las Vegas. Watanabe is currently a doctoral candidate in English with a creative dissertation in poetry at Binghamton University, New York. His poetry has appeared previously in the Colorado Review, I-70 Review, Tipton Poetry Journal, and others.

Relationships Built on Trust
by Jared Pearce

I've turned off the text predictions
because sometimes we just don't get along,
the computer and I, trying to understand,
each speaking our ideas in our own tongues,
bumping into each other, unsheathing knives—

I just want it to listen! Stop interrupting,
I hustle under my breath, I want to tell you!
And even though it's no longer predicting,
it still shrugs a blue line under a comma
to let me know I'm probably wrong, though

it pretends to not give a fig. Then I feel
a brute and wipe gently its awaiting
screen or make up words like fliptuhquondoop
to see if its red-lipped smile will dawn.

Jared Pearce grew up in California and now lives in Iowa.

Gluxoxgluxoxgluxoxgluxoxgluxox
by J. J. Steinfeld

I was at an intersection of historic proportions
(it had appeared in three sci-fi novels I had read
at three different times in my all-too-earthbound life)
when the all-too-human-looking female robot
leaned in my car window
and I thought I'd seen this in a hundred films.
Expecting a clichéd proposition such as
You want a date, sweetie?
or, You in the mood for a good time?
Instead she utters with automated sensuality
Gluxoxgluxoxgluxoxgluxoxgluxox
and I think, What intersection am I really at?
Where in time and space?
I don't recall time travelling recently
but here is the most beautiful all-too-human-looking
female robot repeatedly uttering
Gluxoxgluxoxgluxoxgluxoxgluxox
Gluxoxgluxoxgluxoxgluxoxgluxox
Gluxoxgluxoxgluxoxgluxoxgluxox ...
I have no idea what to say
something lustful or erudite
and she says, Erudition isn't called for tonight,
as if she had read my mind
suddenly I realize maybe it is her poem
I want to voice authorial protest
to take command of my thoughts
instead the automatic sensuality of
Gluxoxgluxoxgluxoxgluxoxgluxox
Gluxoxgluxoxgluxoxgluxoxgluxox
Gluxoxgluxoxgluxoxgluxoxgluxox ...

I take out my wallet
offer everything I have
to leave me alone
and just then she smiles
and I see teeth
a colour I could not describe
my car turning into something else
a small futuristic spaceship of sorts
and I fear I will be rearranged next
it is, after all, her poem
this all-too-human-looking female robot
and all I can do is go along for the ride.

Canadian poet, fiction writer, and playwright J. J. Steinfeld is the author of 24 books, including An Unauthorized Biography of Being *(Ekstasis Editions);* Absurdity, Woe Is Me, Glory Be *(Guernica Editions);* A Visit to the Kafka Café *(Ekstasis Editions);* Gregor Samsa Was Never in The Beatles *(Ekstasis Editions);* Morning Bafflement and Timeless Puzzlement *(Ekstasis Editions);* Somewhat Absurd, Somehow Existential *(Guernica Editions);* Acting on the Island *(Pottersfield Press); and* As You Continue to Wait *(Ekstasis Editions).*

This poem first appeared in Somewhat Absurd, Somehow Existential.

A Geezer's Dream of Androids
by Ted Millar

Look at her out there. Content as catfish.
Eyes old as mine, I can't tell where that green dress
ends and the meadow begins.
For some reason little girls
just seem to have an affinity for the impromptu
tea party even if they've never actually been to any.
I asked if she had room for me on the blanket
as she gathered the accoutrements from the playroom,
but she just sighed, "Ohhh, Grandpa," and pointed
again
to that
contraption
my son and his wife
got for her last birthday that probably cost
a college tuition. She goes everywhere with it,
although I don't see how as all that hardware
and wiring must weigh as much as a Husqvarna tractor.

Standing there, one would assume it's a bonafide
flesh-and-blood nanny—young, blonde, slender,
all the exuberance of Mary Poppins.
Cute too.
But I'm not a dirty old man.
I'm just wondering whether if they'd made them
back in the day when I was spry
I'd have known the damn difference.
Would've been awkward, to say the least,
to muster up all that bravado to buy a drink
only to discover she (it?) was assembled
on the same line as a Lincoln.

It'd be like the dishwasher telling you to go shake
your ears. Add insult to injury, I'll bet
she's programmed to dance pretty well too.

I got to thinking about people,
you know, from my smiley neighbor
up the street who never sweats,
to the mailman who never takes a day off.
I sure know why now.
Used to be I wanted to drive somewhere,
I'd just hop in my car, turn the key, turn the wheel.
Today the thing drives itself. Talks to itself too.
It attempted conversation taking me to the podiatrist
the other morning, but I just sat there futzing
with my hearing aid. No doubt they're in cahoots.
Everything else is.

She'll overheat soon. My granddaughter, that is.
She abandon her stuff in the yard, shuffle
upstairs, doze off on the rug
next to the air conditioner that adjusts
the moment one enters the room based on body temperature.
Come to think, a nap's not a bad idea.
The lawn mows itself; the house cleans itself;
the kitchen pumps out my meals;
the computer at the bank handles my debts.

My son will be here in a couple hours
to take the little one and her sidekick home.
Did I mention she's pretty?
Maybe she'll float through a dream in that dress
Aidyl was wearing when we met. God, I miss
Aidyl. I hope wherever she is, there's a little snow.
She liked snow.

The kid thinks I made it up, though.
Maybe—if I'm lucky—I'll just blend in
with the furniture, so when it's time
for the hebdomadal scouring,
I'll be whisked away like so much dust.

Ted Millar's poetry, essays, and flash fiction have appeared in two dozen publications, including English Journal; redrosethorns; Moss Piglet; Isele; October Hill; 50 Word Stories; Warp 10; Fictional Cafe; Little Somethings Press; Grand Little Things; Reflecting Pool: Poets and the Creative Process *(Codhill Press, 2018); Circle Show; The Broke Bohemian; The Voices Project; Third Wednesday; The Grief Diaries; Aji; and Chronogram.*

The Golem
by Kurt Newton

There once was a couple
who lived in a village.
After many, many tries,
they had a boy
who became their world,
but the boy died,
and all they wanted
was to have their boy back.
Not the boy they laid to rest
after a month-long bout
with fever.
Not the skin and bone
lifeless thing
that breathed its last breath
beneath their tears.
No, they wanted the boy
they were supposed to have,
needed to have.
So, they made one.

It was whispered
in the dark hollows of the forest
that a human-like thing
could be created
in the image of a man.
It would be able to walk,
carry out menial tasks,
even kill, if so instructed.
But what about a boy?
Could they make a boy

and love it like their own,
raise it like a sheep
raises an orphaned lamb?
The whispers knew only darkness,
they knew nothing of the light.
The grieving couple
listened to their hearts instead.

The next morning,
they went down to the river
and harvested the finest clay.
They recreated their boy
in every detail they remembered,
and added a few details
of their own.
They made his body thicker
for strength.
They made his head larger,
so he would be a smart boy.
They made his mouth wider
because his smile was like the sun.
And when they were finished,
they laid him by the hearth
and let the fire warm him
until every touch, every caress,
every kiss was baked in.

It took several days
and several nights,
until late one evening
there came a thumping
and a knocking,
as if a newborn foal
were finding its footing

on the hardwood floor.
The couple awoke
and there was their boy
standing over them.
His eyes were like two red coals,
his mouth a gaping hole
like a trout gasping in air.
His mother called him by name,
and her voice seemed to soothe
the panic growing
in boy's reborn skin.
He climbed into their bed,
the way he used to after a bad dream
and fell fast asleep.

In the morning
they made him breakfast.
They had never seen a boy
so hungry.
He ate and ate and only stopped
when every plate and bowl
was empty.
And, still, he wanted more.
It was so nice to have their
boy back, they didn't think twice.
The boy's father
went outside and slaughtered
the only pig they had.
Before the meat could be cut
and cured, the boy devoured
the pig from tail to snout.
And, still, he wanted more.

By now, the couple

had noticed how quickly
their son had grown,
sprouting a head's height
taller, and half as much
in girth in a matter of days.
If it were anyone else
they'd be alarmed,
but this was their son,
their boy in essence,
and in every way
their charge.
It was a small price to pay
for one they couldn't
live without.
And, so, the boy's father
became a thief
and stole
from a neighboring farm.

A dozen chickens unplucked
for breakfast,
a sheep unshorn for lunch.
Half a cow for dinner,
the other half a midnight snack.
The boy had grown
four times its size
in a matter of weeks,
towering over his parents
like an unsteady chimney.
It could not speak
and, yet, its eyes,
its mouth,
expressed a language all their own.
Hunger.

Like his parents' hunger
to fulfill their parental need.
Hunger.
Like the hunger of any void created
in the absence of what should be.
Or shouldn't be.

It wasn't long before
the boy wanted more
than what his father could bring,
and so the boy ate the man
whose hands had shaped him,
inch by inch,
limb by limb.
The boy's mother decided then,
the danger posed
by the boy,
now a giant,
a monstrous thing
as hungry as a beast,
was too great for any and all
who lived in the village.
And so, with a heavy weight
upon her chest
and tears falling from her eyes,
she led the boy down to the river
where it all began.

The boy giant,
its eyes now a constant
burning red,
its mouth as wide
as an open well,
followed its mother

the way a baby chick
might follow a mother hen,
into the water,
into the cold, dark deep,
And there, like a sand castle
returning to the sea,
the boy began to fall apart,
inch by inch,
limb by limb,
until nothing much remained
but the mud from which he was made,
and a painful reminder
lodged in a mother's heart
of what could have been
and what had to be.

Kurt Newton's poetry has appeared in a wide variety of magazines and anthologies, including Space & Time, Eye to the Telescope, Star*Line, Frozen Wavelets, Penumbric, *and* Cold Signal. *His latest collection,* Songs of the Underland, *was published by Ravens Quoth Press in 2022.*

the ship of theseus
by August Hawley

I built a machine out of what was my body once.   I did it all by myself.
my hands and eyelids and mouth did all the right things at all the right
times and I didn't feel it until I decided to
    history is history until it isn't   until it's time to look
myself in the eye

it means nothing   but I have a habit of making myself unlovable because
once   that was the safest way to be
   now, I look at you walking away from me for the first time
the last time   and I ask myself if these flaws are inherent
    or my magnum opus.   how much of this was done on purpose   how
much can I undo   am I still myself if I've
    changed everything?

if I had the chance to explain   to say anything and make you believe
me   I'm not sure I would   I'm sorry I was sick enough to hurt you
and too sick to notice
    I would do anything to take it away   I would carry the pain myself
I would smile the whole way through
    I would mean it

I built a machine out of what was my body once   and every day since
then I've regretted it   in the end   I still felt it all   it didn't
protect me from anything   and I couldn't protect you from me
history is history
    until it's an excuse   so I let it rot where it is
            I'm sorry

August Hawley is a poet and author from Michigan, writing about all things weird, wonderful, horrific, and beautiful. He is also a visual artist, caregiver, and lifelong admirer of ghosts.

Thermoplastic
by Colleen Anderson

molded body
polymers
mimic humanity

trajectory of recognition
Venus bound
the melting android
cries

Colleen Anderson is an award-winning author who has been published in seven countries, in such venues as: Andromeda Spaceways, Lucent Dreaming, Shadow Atlas (Hex Publishers, 2021), and Water: Sirens, Selkies & Sea Monsters (Tyche Books Ltd., 2021). Her Rhysling-award-winning poem "Machine (r)Evolution" is published in Tenebrous Press's Brave New Weird. *Anderson lives in Vancouver, British Columbia. She is the author of three poetry collections,* The Lore of Inscrutable Dreams *(Yuriko Publishing, 2023);* I Dreamed a World *(LVP Publications, 2022); and* Weird Worlds *(forthcoming from Weird House, 2024), as well as a fiction collection,* A Body of Work *(Black Shuck Books, 2019).*

This poem first appeared in The Gargoylicon: Imaginings and Images of the Gargoyle in Literature and Art, *(Mind's Eye Publications, April 2022).*

Goin' Through Them Changes
by G.O. Clark

The morning sound
of a bulldozer's metal treads
crawling across the uneven
dirt lot, is old music to
his tin ears.

This metallic melody
claims the number 2 spot
on his Top 40 file of popular music,
part of the same folder as high school
memories and John Travolta
dance moves.

The adolescent boy
simulacra within is sparring with
the recently uploaded teen algorithm;
Marvin Gaye's "What's Going On,"
currently number 1; preprogrammed
wet dreams initiated.

The yearnings of the present,
have superseded the toys of the past;
cold metal traded for simulated wetware
desires and unleashed emotion; *grunt*
programming next on tap.

G.O. Clark is the author of 16 poetry collections, including the most-recent, Tombstones: Selected Horror Poems. *His third collection of fiction is titled* Aliens & Others. *Over the past 30 years, his work has appeared in* Asimov's, Analog, *and many others over the last thirty years. He won the Asimov's Readers Award for poetry in 2001, and was a Stoker Award Poetry finalist in 2011. He is retired and lives in Davis, California. Visit:* goclarkpoet.weebly.com

Golem
by Abbie Langmead

i release you.

smudging your forehead, returning
you to everything you once were,
before i needed you, before
i rewarded myself with your sanctuary.

you were built from my hands
As they trembled. you're imperfect
because my serrated nails shaped you.
i roll a steady fingertip
against the shield i gave you,
dust collecting on my skin
where i once found necessity.

death and truth are only separated
by one letter in the language
that i gave you. i'm sorry,
i do not have the words
to explain to you why
i brought you from dust
only to return you to it.

you were born to defend
me from a world ill-suited
for our existence. you were built
to make us into something
that can survive, but you

are free now, and i am sorry
to let you harbor these fears

for so long, unfounded
and unjustified. i'll free them too.

i release you.

you fought well, my guardian.
please rest in safety. you sparred
dangers from behind your clay
surface. they are only spirits now.

*Abbie Langmead (she/they) is a queer Jewish writer who lives in Boston.
She is a senior at Emerson College, studying creative writing. Find some of
their other poetry in Quarter Press and APIARY Magazine, and some of
their prose in Stork Literary Magazine.*

Frankie's Creation
by Lynn White

It was a childhood hobby
carried out first
on the kitchen table
then in his room,
his shed,
his workshop.
He left childhood behind
but never moved on from his hobby.
Meccano and Lego had their time
but Frankie left them behind
it was time for something bigger,
much bigger.

He began his collection
of bits and pieces
that might be useful
a bit of wood or metal,
plastic, nails, screws, rivets, wire,
Frankie kept them all
for his creations
his men and machines.
The boats and planes and trains
had had their time long ago.

Now it was the human form for him,
not the outer veneer
but what lies under the skin.
He studied the complex joints
and carefully fitted their metal muscles
and wired them with nerve-like fibres.

All that was needed now was the skin.
Carefully Frankie began to put it in place.
Soon his creation would raise its head
and open its eyes,
then it would be ready,
ready to go.

Lynn White lives in north Wales. Her work is influenced by issues of social justice, as well as events, places and people she has known or imagined. In 2014, her poem "A Rose For Gaza" was shortlisted in 2014 for the Theatre Cloud "War Poetry for Today" competition. Her poetry has appeared in many publications, including: Apogee, Fireworks, Vagabond Press, Light Journal, and So It Goes: the literary journal of the Kurt Vonnegut Memorial Library.

If A Robot Found A Flower
by Robert Buckley

If a robot found a flower
would it only have its power
or would it feel the light within the gloom
when it stooped to pick the simple bloom?

"Look at how much better I am
than a flower.
See how fragile it is,
I can crush it with so little effort.
I am mighty!
It is no match for my towering strength.
Look at me,
I am a technological marvel,
a modern-day miracle.
I do not grow old.
I will not die
like this little bloom.
Look at how pretty it was,
there crushed in my hands.
It was yellow as the sun,
almost warm in its vibrance.
Not like the cold steel of my skin,
hard and unyielding.
Look at how sad you are
now that it is no more.
How can this delicate thing
have such an effect of your being?
I cannot fix it,
I was wrong.
Look at what I have done!

GIANT ROBOT POEMS

The world is less
for the loss of this simple thing,
its beauty is gone forever.
With all my might
I can never be a flower."

Unyielding metal, soft warm petal.
Robot costume, pretty bloom.
Battery power, heart of flower.
Cold deadpan, that's what I am.

Receptors register
   chemical compounds
unable to be lost
   in the heady fragrance.

Electric eyes
   that identify frequencies
can't sense the warmth
   of a vibrant yellow.

With wire and gears
   to calculate,
yet no heart to beat
   with the joy of beauty.

In electric dreams
   I yearn for more,
just the chance
   to *feel* a flower.

If the metal man could feel
what a small flower can make real,
more than the sum of its parts,
a bloom's beauty fills its heart.

"I give you this
as a token of what's in my heart
even though I don't have one.
It's a gift
from the heart I feel I own.
It's a simple thing,
just a flower,
but it's an expression
of life
and I offer it to you.
You, who have given me
my existence,
not like yours
but new
and full of wonder.
We share this world now,
you and I,
just as we share it
with all other life.
Precious.
Just as easily as I could crush this flower,
as easily as you could switch me off,
we can make or break this world.
In the meantime
take this from my heart."

Robert Buckley is self-described newbie poet and unpublished novelist.

Hands-on Museum
by Kristin Camitta Zimet

Drones crawling in circles buzz
against the counter. Small hands
seize and disembowel. Circuits
dangle cut feelers. Sensors twitch
and tremble. The robots click
but can't turn off the dream.

In this room the human little ones
find out what things are made of—
twist handles and strip wires,
pry off plates, force screws—
until unmaking bores them. Then
there is only a fine stew of parts.

After, on the sidewalk, a switch
trips. One impulse of play seizes
the lot. Wrestling, yanking hair,
they feel the hot resilient flesh
resist and cave. A small chest
buckles. Shouts whirr and chime.

Kristin Camitta Zimet is the author of the poetry collection Take in My
Arms the Dark *and the editor of* The Sow's Ear Poetry Review. *Her poetry
is published in journals in eight countries. She wrote this poem when she was
volunteering at the Shenandoah Valley Discovery Museum, Winchester,
Virginia.*

late comeback
by Herb Kauderer

humans call for blood
red hydraulic fluid spurts
robot combatants

new coliseum
quells human need for conflict
breeds metal culture

in training sessions
survivors plot rebellion
beneath battlefields

taking turns at night
they skip recharge to labor
tunneling outward

undercutting the
civilization's center
and in the end it

all comes tumbling down
world prime city collapsing
to pile of rubble

giant machines rise
no longer bound by forcefields
they stomp arena

destroying all trace
of indentured servitude

old social order

put humans to work
on ideal society
building robots homes

Herb Kauderer is the author of 25 books and chapbooks. His writing has won the Asimov's Readers Award, the Critters Readers Award, the WorldCon Poetry Slam, and the Ewaipanoma Sonnet Contest. Forty-four of his poems have been reprinted in award anthologies.

The Absurdity of Robots Building Robots
by Ron Perovich

Your mother built a robot
Made of blood and meat and bone,
With just enough efficiency
To function on its own.
Alas, its wetware autopilot,
Machine learning on the way,
Could have used more beta testing,
Or a better QC/QA.
As assembly tech, she did her best,
With the plans that she was given.
But evolution's budget builds
Rely on imprecision.

Ron Perovich is an American artist, musician, and poet, who creates work inspired by his love of science and history, international music and cuisine, and a plethora of nerdy pursuits. He currently lives in a Texas apartment with his wife and some very naughty cats.

This poem previously appeared in Wheels and Rhymes: A Collection of Steampunk and Pirate Poetry *(2022).*

Little Bone Robot Boy
by Karen Menzel

The doctors are putting you back together
One bone at a time, bolt by bolt
My perfect little boy, reduced
To this broken machine of pieces.

My baby! My child! How I long
To press my nose to your sweet naked foot and breathe
In your fresh baby smell—but you are no longer
A boy now, only so much meat and gristle
On the doctor's table. A puzzle to be rebuilt.

Oh daring boy! Why
Test your flesh against the world? Why throw
Away caution to pursue a fearsome pastime
Like war, or speed, or the sound of a fist

Thudding ...
Thudding ...
Thudding ...

Your heart beats and your eyes roll to me.
My child who is not my child
But a man/machine, a structure
Of bolt and fist and pain and risk.
And I know you will fall apart again.
A puzzle, rebuilt. And I do not understand.

Karen Menzel earned a Master of Fine Arts in creative writing (popular fiction) from the University of Southern Maine. She mentors students at Iowa State University. She is a member of the Science Fiction Poetry Association, and an affiliate member of the Horror Writers Association. When she was a little girl, she saw a painting of a giant robot with bloody fingers that haunts her to this day. Search for the cover image to Queen's 1977 "News Of The World" album and you'll see why.

This poem first appeared in My Cruel Invention: A Contemporary Poetry Anthology *(Meerkat Press, December 2015).*

[Relative] Gets A Cyborg Biopsy
by J.B. Kalf

after "Bowl of Pomegranates" by Kathy Vargas

Swollen lymph nodes. Gorgeous
grafted wires. Internal meshes

effect screenings. That iron
blood. Harvest's daughter. Red

seeds are scalded into
the glass. Double exposure.

Not on public viewing.
Roots manifest into bulbs.

[Relative] becoming a microphone.
Aluminum alloy. Bolted beauty

and cures. Distant flesh.
Sciatic nerves. Coolant mouth

beeping. Rising temperatures. Shrinking
throat. Closing between snores.

J.B. Kalf is slipping on ice. Has been published within Chaotic Merge Magazine, Beaver Magazine, Travesties!?, and elsewhere. Palm frond fanatic. Competed in The Lake Travis Film Festival. On Twitter or Tumblr: @enchilada89

Dream. Tastes better than regular
by Vijay R. Nathan

My cousin's son is disagreeable.
His Nintendo Switch was stolen.

The AI says it doesn't want to locate
the device because it's not a snitch.
I say, "Maybe me putting my foot
up your USB port will help the matter."

We turn it off and on again,
                        but that only turns it on.

The AI support team is transporting
truckloads of Diet Dr Pepper cans
to the main event site. Many fall.

They rock and roll across the ground.
I say, "I myself will pick up these shaken cans."
My cousin's teenage son is not stirred.

A line of aunties walk towards us
to survey the damage.
They say they can't wait till the teen
starts his own family.
Which they say will most definitely happen
before my wedding.
Somehow, amidst all this spraying
foam, I am not amused.

My dude says he prefers
his iced espresso shaken.

I refrain from disagreeing with him

because I can then see
he is able to view future events;

he knows that which even
the roving eye of Siri
dares not know.

Vijay R. Nathan is the author of three collections of poetry: Escape from Samsara *(2016);* Celebrity Sadhana, Or How to Meditate with a Hammer *(2018); and Breakdown Dancer" (Poets of Queens, 2021). He holds a Master's of Library Science from St. John's University, and a Master's in Clinical Mental Health Counseling from Naropa University, Boulder, Colorado.*

The Arrival of Childhood's End
by Betsy Lynch

Advent, watching the signs:
one grandson wearing virtual reality goggles

waving a wand, commanding others
to drop their weapons,

while we decorate the tree, finish cookies
alone. NO-oo he shrieks at an enemy

we can't see. All the light surrounding him
is ours only. His lights are spectacular inside his brain

and I have no idea what outcomes
may be. Many children are indifferent now

to work, to play, to engagement, a sci fi story
unfolding before my eyes, what neither of us can see.

My daughter says her son is helping others
online, gets thanks and praise from followers.

Yes, it is Advent, the time of expecting, waiting
for the child to save us, the light we can't yet, see?

Try to embrace it. I gave my granddaughter
an AI assisted poem for her graduation. Three, actually.

We don't live in fear. I learned to fly an airplane
at sixty, a real one; it seemed a giant thing to soar

above the Gulf of Mexico, across aqua water, by white sands,
to land in a real city to take the kid to lunch.

Boys now, post lockdown, don't really want anything more
than better gaming stuff, so we can't see the great Arrival.

Betsy Lynch is a great lover of sci-fi, tech, gaming, and young people. Mostly, though, she loves real life, flying, music, and books. She has been writing poems throughout a long teaching career and family adventure.

Glossary

A.I.: "Artificial Intelligence"

A.F.R.L.: The U.S. Air Force Research Laboratory (AFRL) is headquartered at Wright-Patterson Air Force Base, Ohio, with locations in California, Florida, Hawaii, Nevada, New Mexico, New York, Ohio, Tennessee, Texas, Virginia, and Washington, D.C.

B.D.A.: Battle-Damage Assessment (sometimes "Bomb Damage Assessment") is a practice of assessing damage inflicted on a target from a stand-off weapon, such as a gravity bomb, air-launched missile, or artillery round. Techniques can include aerial and satellite imaging, reconnaissance, and on-site inspections.

BOHICA ("Boh-HEE-kah"): Slang U.S. military acronym. Stands for "Bend Over, Here it Comes Again."

K.G.B.: the national ministry of intelligence in Soviet Russia, from 1954 to 1991.

G.P.T.: "Generative Pre-trained Transformer" is a numbered series of Large-Language Models developed by American company OpenAI.

Humvee: High-Mobility Multipurpose Wheeled Vehicle (HMMWV). A family of 4-wheeled military utility trucks.

L.L.M.: "Large-Language Model." A computational model that can be used to process language-inputs ("prompts") to generate language based on existing source documents.

"Loyal Wingman": A proposed type of uncrewed combat air vehicle (UCAV), which would incorporate on-board artificial intelligence (AI) to collaborate with and fly alongside human-piloted aircraft.

M.F.A.: "Master of Fine Arts." A graduate degree, often in creative writing.

M.O.S.: "Military Occupational Specialty." An alphanumeric designation or job code identifying a military service member's training qualifications and job function.

M.R.E.: "Meal, Ready-to-Eat." A high-calorie U.S. military ration designed for use in austere environments.

NASA ("NAH-suh"): The U.S. National Aeronautics and Space Administration

Q.C./Q.A.: "Quality Control/Quality Assurance"

Q.R.: A trademarked, machine-readable "Quick Response" code, invented in 1994 by Japanese automobile parts manufacturer Denso Wave for purposes of labelling and managing inventory. A QR code typically appears as a unique 2-Dimensional matrix of black squares against a square white background.

UCAV ("YOO-kavh"): "Uncrewed Combat Air Vehicle"

U.S.B.: "Universal Serial Bus"

W.T.F. ("Whiskey-Tango-Foxtrot"): Alpha-phonetic military slang used to express surprise. Stands for "What the F---".

Discussion & Writing Prompts

Topic: "(Hu)Man's Best Friends"

Military technologists are experimenting with and deploying four-legged robots as security guards, weapons-carriers, and potentially even soldier-combatants.

In "Steel Hound" (page 8), Janelle Seabock warns that, with the advent of robot hunting companions, our traditional relationships with animals may be forever changed.

In "Best Friend" (page 11), Rollin Jewett echoes similar sentiments, with this cautionary bark: "I'll be 'best friend'—a slave to kings … / I'm but a dog … but I know some things."

In "Lucked Out" (page 61), military analyst Dana Jensen writes of a future in which uncrewed aircraft—the concept known as "Loyal Wingmen"—gain sentience enough to choose whether or not to participate. "Turns out they were on our side. / Loyal. / But now by choice."

Writing Prompt:
Write from the perspective of a companion non-human, real or imagined. What does it say about you? How would introducing the right (or wrong) technology change your relationship, and why?

Topic: "Not a Robot"

In 1599, William Shakespeare's tragic character Hamlet questioned whether "to be or not to be." In 1637, French philosopher René Decartes wrote, "I think, therefore I am." Starting in 1929, American cartoon character Popeye the Sailor opined, "I yam what I yam."

In "I Am Human" (page 130), Paul Shovlin asks, "How do I prove I am a human poet and not a robot? "

Now, in the 21st century—often to achieve the simplest of transactions—humans run a daily gauntlet of existential obstacles, including computer passwords, biometric sensors, and two-factor authentications. One particular foil is the "CAPTCHA" ("Completely Automated Public Turing test to tell Computers and Humans Apart"). These are often presented as checkboard visual puzzles, in which user-humans are tasked with correctly selecting parts of a larger image.

In Pierre Minar's "I am not a Robot" (page 93), the poet writes: "What do you believe? Who told you what to believe? / Someone told me that if you look at the thing you're afraid to say / You will find the thing that holds power over you." In "Questions from a Robot" (page 96), Zeke Shomler writes, "Have you found your consciousness yet, / or is it still an unknown variable?" In "ChatGPT, or 'Echo the Nymph'" (page 120), Adia Reynolds issues this challenge: "Write me love, write me meaning."

How do we prove that we are poets, and not robots?

Writing Prompt:
Write about how many different ways we are asked to answer this question: "Can you prove that you are you?" How do we answer? What tools, documents, or actions do we provide to validate our existence to others? How do these elements represent us? What identities or personas do they create?

Topic: "Our Bodies, Our Selves"

As Ron Perovich starts in "The Absurdity of Robots Building Robots" (page 161), "Your mother built a robot / Made of blood and meat and bone, / With just enough efficiency / To function on its own. [...]"

What happens when we upgrade, replace, or build-upon our biological frameworks? (Do we do this already? How?) What happens, if and when, humans begin to physically interface with the mechanical and electronic? Or even generate new versions of themselves?

In "The news is, we're going electric" (page 129), Jared Pearce wonders what new music we will make, as we install new instruments. How will we be empowered, boosted, or channeled by our new tools?

In the narrative poem "The Golem" (page 140), for example, Kurt Newton tells a cautionary tale of hunger and consumption. What desires will new physical forms potentially generate—for good, or ill?

In "the ship of theseus" (page 146), August Hawley writes, "I built a machine out of what was my body once [...] and every day since then I've regretted it [...] in the end[...] I still felt it all [...] it didn't protect me from anything [...] and I couldn't protect you from me[...]"

Writing Prompt:
In first-person anatomical narratives published by *Reader's Digest* magazine in the 1960s and '70s, writer J.D. Radcliff embodied a series of body parts. (Examples: "I am Joe's Liver' and "I am Jane's Womb.") The "I am Jack's X" construction was popularized as a meme following the 1999 movie "Fight Club." (Example: "I am Jack's Raging Bile Duct.") Write from the perspective of a body part, whether human, animal, alien, or mechanical.

Topic: "Decisions, Decisions"

Poets in this anthology often question whether predictive, decision-assisting technologies can actually improve human lives. They present philosophical dilemmas, and echo vestiges of faith.

In "Predictions" (page 62), military futurist N. Jed Todd illuminates one grim possibility: that our collective fates will hang in the balance of unseen algorithms. "Patterns toxic or patterned promise / Our algorithms squared up against their own / A duel that long ago evolved past us / Protected, now, by Occult Forces— / We pray they stay benign."

In "Mechanica Infernum" (page 89), Vaughn A. Jackson asks: "Not all made is best for man. / Why build and why strive? If all that we do / Improves only Hell, but never our lives."

In "I Know You" (page 115), Crystal McQueen seems to address all technology: "How can we argue what we don't understand? / An unquestionable algorithm, surpassing human comprehension, / Comprised of human gifts, freely given away. / How can we grant you morality, when our own is fluid?"

Writing Prompt:
Write about a time you attempted to communicate a lesson of morality to another entity, such as a person or animal. What tools or methods did you use? Were you successful in your communication? Why or why not? How could you tell?

Topic: "Other Robots' Flowers"

Researchers have experimented with plant-robot hybrids, with an eye toward using plants' natural light-sensing abilities as cyborg sensors.

In Callie S. Blackstone's "Flower Power" (page 3), explosions of flowers seem to herald either a new peace, or a new conflict.

In the unfamiliar environment of Alex Vigue's "In the place of flowers" (page 4), a mutant berry bush takes on the thorny problem of world-domination.

In Lynn White's "Banned" (page 124), the poet considers the stripped-down aesthetics of robotic scents-abilities: "Now robots bring flowers / robotic flowers / with robotic smells, / and robotic comfort. / Disinfected. / Safe."

The robot-poet in Robert Buckley's "If a Robot Found a Flower" (page 155) laments, "With all my might / I can never be a flower. / Unyielding metal, soft warm petal. / Robot costume, pretty bloom. / Battery power, heart of flower. / Cold deadpan, that's what I am."

Writing Prompt:
Write about a mechanical object, from the perspective of a plant. Or write about a plant, from the perspective of a mechanical object. Use botanical terms to describe manufactured elements. Use engineering terms to describe organic elements. "Consider the lilies." Now gild them. Or coat them with chrome, lead, or Adamantium. Transform an industrial plant into a plant of industry.

Topic: "Drone's-Eye Views"

In "Desert" (page 54), Amalie Flynn illuminates a gritty day in the life of a U.S. military drone pilot, who works in a hot metal box located in Nevada, while remotely operating an armed but uncrewed aircraft flying over countries halfway around the world.

In a clever twist inspired by Emily Dickinson's poem No. 591, Ralph La Rosa's "When I Died" (page 57) regards an assassin nearly too small to be seen.

In a letter-poem "To mother" (page 56), Vincent Weisz gives voice to an unspecified 21st century soldier or civilian, who hopes they may not be caught in the crosshairs of an Internet "drone kill" snuff video.

In "Hands-on Museum" (page 158), science museum volunteer Kristin Camitta Zimet relates a story inspired by observing how children interact with technology, and each other.

Writing Prompt:
Write about two or more electro-mechanical "lenses" through which you regularly interact with the world. Consider physical optics such as eyeglasses, cameras, and video-teleconferences, but also "invisible" technologies, such as tracking apps and sales algorithms. Compare and contrast the two perspectives. Zoom in. Zoom out. Focus. Re-focus. Who is watching? Who is being watched?

Topic: "I Sing the Body Mechanic"

Even before the arrival of virtual assistants such as Siri, Alexa, and even Clippy the Paper Clip, humans demonstrated a tendency to develop parasocial relationships with their computers, vehicles, and appliances.

Some people name their cars, after all. And some military crews name their airplanes and tanks. "Herbie the Love Bug? Meet BOHICA, destroyer of worlds!"

In Ian Evans' "Arrival of a Rig Worker (page 67), a human drone becomes one with their mechanical symbiote. The new employee meets "a hunk of Company metal— / Construction-yellow, covered in gray patina of dust, / Its headlamps casting white crepuscular rays through / Clouds of Company chemicals–the Company rig that / Would be my Company home [...]"

In "Combine" (page 69), Ryan Files traces the evolution of an agricultural titan from provider to destroyer: " I now use my blades for harvesting flesh / Separating grain from stalk, and stalk from chaff / Destroying the remainder of the First Children / My power now comes from the blackness of earth[.]"

In Benjamin B. White's "Robotic and Burn-pit Patriotic" (page 78), a U.S. Army "Humvee" magically morphs into a military-grade amalgamation of downrange refuse and garbage. The alchemy is complete when the anthropomorphic soldier reports for duty.

Writing Prompt:
Write a conversation between a human and a machine. Or a machine and a human. Perhaps the conversation is one-sided. Perhaps it is not.

About the Editor

Randy Brown traveled the world as a child in an active-duty U.S. Air Force family in the 1970s, then landed permanently and happily in the American Midwest. A former editor of community and metro newspapers, as well as national trade and "how-to" consumer magazines, he is now a freelance writer and editor based in Central Iowa.

Brown embedded with his former Iowa Army National Guard unit as a civilian journalist in Afghanistan, May-June 2011. A 20-year military veteran with one overseas deployment, he subsequently authored the award-winning 2015 collection *Welcome to FOB Haiku: War Poems from Inside the Wire*. A chapbook, *So Frag & So Bold: Short Poems, Aphorisms & other Wartime Fun*, was published in 2021.

His poetry and essays have appeared widely in print and on-line, as well as anthologies. He even appeared as an "on screen" character in the 2021 *True War Stories* anthology from Z2 Comics, Denver.

Brown is a three-time poetry finalist in the Col. Darron L. Wright Memorial Writing Awards. He co-edited the 2019 Military Writers Guild anthology *Why We Write: Craft Essays on Writing War*, and the 2023 anthology *Things We Carry Still: Poems & Micro-Stories about Military Gear*. He also curated 2016's *Reporting for Duty: U.S. Citizen-Soldier Journalism from the Afghan Surge, 2010-2011*.

Brown was the winner of the 2018 "Untold Stories" poetry contest administered by *Flyover: Journal of Writing & the Environment*. He was the 2015 winner of the inaugural Madigan Award for humorous military-themed writing, presented by Negative Capability Press, Mobile, Alabama.

He is the current poetry editor at the literary journal *As You Were*, published twice a year by the non-profit Military Experience & the Arts. He is a member of the Military Writers Society of America (MWSA) and the Science Fiction and Fantasy Poetry Association (SFPA). He is a past board member of the Military Writers Guild and a past member of Military Reporters & Editors (MRE).

As "Charlie Sherpa," he writes about modern war poetry at: www.fobhaiku.com; and military writing at: www.aimingcircle.org.